Bond of Trust

Marc Livingstone

Copyright © James Livingstone 2023

The moral right of the author has been asserted

This is a work of fiction. Names, characters, places and incidents are either the product of the author's imagination or are used fictitiously, and any resemblance to actual persons, living or dead, business establishments, companies, events or places is entirely coincidental

Thank you Shelley

Chapter 1

The call had come in late at night. There was a rather irritated voice on the other end. 'Is that Mike Stone? I've been trying to get you all day. Where have you been?' It took a moment to realise it was Toby Jones from Naval Command.

'And a good evening to you too, Toby.'

'Sorry, it's just that I've left you lots of messages. Don't you check your phone?'

'What can I do for you at this late hour, Toby?'

'An urgent job. A mine has popped up in Gumerston, a salmon fishing estate in the Western Isles. Colonel Bentley is the head of their fishing syndicate and knows my commanding officer, so I've been getting some earache about fixing this fast. He tells me they have Prince John coming up, so they're getting rather anxious and thinking they'll have to cancel unless we can get it cleared.'

'It's a sea mine, yes? I thought salmon fishing was in rivers and freshwater lochs?'

'True, but he's coming by seaplane and needs to land in the sea estuary in front of their fishing lodge.'

'Can't he alter his travel plans like a normal person?'

'No. He's just been fishing on his godfather's estate on the west coast of Ireland and is flying up in his new toy.'

'So, no customs for the prince?'

'No, I think they still believe Ireland is part of their kingdom, so he's officially arriving a week later. I'm told the usual bigwigs are going to be there, including some lords as well as Earl Cooper and the Courier newspaper owners, so they don't want to be looking like fools if he can't land safely. Apparently, it's his first time coming and everything needs to be perfect.'

'Where are they?'

'Tumelray, an island between Skye and the Outer Hebrides.'

'God, isn't that the island the Sunday Courier wrote about that "time forgot"? Something about a religious group that resisted modern technology until they were hit by typhoid or something, and the Scottish government had to intervene in the eighties? That's miles away. Is there a ferry? When does he arrive?'

'Next week, Wednesday sometime. Yes, if you get up there tonight, you can catch the ferry. They have two crossings each week in the summer.'

'Okay, I think we can get on the road right away. Just need to check with Dave and tell him to pack his kilt. Send us a photo if you can, so we know what type of mine we're dealing with.'

Mike gave Dave a call.

'Bloody hell, I was going to do the Solway Coast marathon on Saturday. Prince John, what's he, third or fourth in line for the throne, or are they counting women these days?'

Mike texted Toby, 'Good to go.'

The equipment was nearly all ready. Most of it was brand new, apart from Dave's treasured and slightly battered old green Land Rover, as the business was just a few months old. Dave had set it up when he left the Navy, as he knew with cutbacks he could get lots of work as a private contractor doing the same job he'd just been doing for the Royal Navy, but for a lot more money and plenty time off to spend with his daughter, Poppy.

Mike had met Dave while taking part in a trail run across Hadrian's Wall, going coast to coast, and they had hit it off straightaway after taking a wrong turn, running an extra fifteen miles across the moor and then working together to get back on track. Dave had persuaded Mike to stop teaching science and technology and join him in this new adventure.

The new logo, 'MineTrade,' on the side of the boat, had just been pencilled in, ready for painting, and the new mini-sub was in the back of the Land Rover, looking like a torpedo all strapped down. It was a new piece of kit and had cost a small fortune, but it was proving invaluable at, among other things, identifying strings of mines through its sonar, infrared, sensors and cameras, all fed back to a laptop.

Their Boxer dog was woken from a deep sleep and, with one eye open, climbed into her bed, which had been thrown into the back of the vehicle along with her dog food. She promptly fell asleep again as Mike turned the key in the ignition and they were on their way. She always came on UK trips as the best car and kit anti-theft device. Mike hadn't been able to decide on a name for her when she was a puppy, so she just became Boxer.

When they picked Dave up, he was still less than happy at missing the Solway coast marathon, but he was wearing an appropriate tartan shirt.

Heading up to the west coast of Scotland on a wet windy cold night seemed in keeping with recent journeys. The blower in the Land Rover barely cleared the screen of condensation, so the vents were left open and thick jackets had to be worn. The windscreen wipers were all but useless in the persistent torrential rain the west of Scotland was throwing down at them. The heater was set to full, but it just made one knee very hot and did little else. According to Dave, this Land Rover was 'a classic.' At least the traffic was clear at this time of night.

The journey was long and monotonous, and their concentration ebbed and waned as they stared into the black of the night as the wind tried on occasion to push them off the road. Boxer snored for a lot of the journey, as if attached to an amplifier at times. The men had a heart-stopping moment when a stag crossed the road at about half-past three in Glen Coe; it was like a ghost coming into sharp focus as it stopped and looked straight at them for a moment before continuing on its journey.

Mike had thought the journey up may be an opportunity to discuss how Dave was feeling after the death of his wife, Jenny. She had wanted Dave to leave the Navy and stop doing bomb disposal because she feared that one day it might be his last. On the day he did leave, his brother greeted him at the railway station to tell him the tragic news. Jenny had died earlier that day when a car had run a red light trying to evade a chasing police car, hitting her vehicle side-on while it was waiting for the traffic light to turn green.

Dave's coping mechanism in the proceeding months seemed to be to go out running even more than the five days he regularly ran, often at night, and Mike was worried an already thin Dave was losing too much weight and would burn out; but when Mike raised his concerns, Dave only talked about his improved PBs. Dave had only opened up to Mike once about Jenny's death after a couple of whiskies, which was all it took to get Dave drunk, as he only occasionally drank alcohol and weighed about 140 lbs. He had fallen apart in a sobbing mess, blaming himself for not quitting sooner and saying he should have told her not to pick him up from the railway station. Dave couldn't speak highly enough of the teachers that had helped Poppy when she'd returned to school. Since then, Dave had been deft at avoiding speaking about the subject ever again. Mike tried to broach it by starting a conversation about Jenny as the morning light broke through, but he empathetically sensed it wasn't the right time and instead asked about Dave's daughter, who was away at an expensive boarding school – one considerable perk of being deployed abroad; recently it had mainly been in the South China Sea, working from the aircraft carrier the *Queen Elizabeth*.

'How's Poppy? Is she having a good summer term?'

'Yes, she seems to love school. She'll be home in a week. I promised her I'd teach her to dive this summer.'

'Just take her somewhere warm, or she may hate it,' suggested Mike.

Six hours later, the Land Rover arrived at the ferry port with two hours to spare. The rain had stopped, and the sea was glass-like – a surprise, given the recent storms. The sun was breaking through the early morning mist like a Turner painting. The familiar smell of sea ozone was distinct but subtle, and the seagulls were relatively quiet. Maybe this was the lull before the storm.

Boxer was alert and curious as to where they had arrived this time. Dave had been very reluctant; anticipating chaos when Mike had originally suggested Boxer could join them on jobs, but he had relented after the first week, as Boxer seemed to be taking her new job very seriously. Her only slip-up in the last year was chewing the tail of a lobster Dave had thrown in the back of the Land Rover for dinner after one dive.

A photo pinged up on Mike's phone as they arrived and got mobile reception back, with a message from Toby, thanking them. It looked like the standard sea mine every WWII film shows. Decades later, they were still showing up – not surprising really, as over 50,000 were laid in the Baltic alone, never mind the north Atlantic barrage; those were laid from the Orkneys to Norway, although nearly all of them were now lying on the ocean floor.

The ferry journey was without incident, a godsend compared to the last one Mike had done; that time it was to Lewis and had lasted eighteen hours. When the ferry had left the harbour, it had found the sea too rough to dock at Stornaway. It had then tried to return to the harbour at Ullapool, only to find it too rough to dock there too, so it was forced to stay in a nearby sheltered bay for the next ten hours. Mike remembered starting to turn green.

As they got in the Land Rover to disembark, Mike turned the key, but the engine was dead – nothing at all; it wasn't even trying to start. The two men checked the engine to find the heavy rain had penetrated almost everywhere. They got a jump start from a fellow Land Rover owner, but a new battery or starter motor was going to be needed.

Mike realised they weren't going to make it to the fishing lodge that night. He called Toby to let him know and was pleasantly surprised to find him more relaxed compared to the last call. Toby explained that they couldn't have worked on a Sunday anyway, as the whole island was 'God-squad' mad, and he said he would update Colonel Bentley on their new ETA.

Getting a room this late on a Saturday was going to be difficult, but it was preferable to a tent with storms and midges about. However, they quickly found that nobody they called wanted to let out a room on a Saturday night. The Sabbath seemed to be a very big deal here.

Eventually, Mike and Dave found a B&B run by some outsiders or, as the locals called them, 'Sassenachs.'

The guest house was clean but basic; the welcome was curt. It appeared to be the guest's privilege to give them their money to stay there. The dog couldn't come in, and they were warned they couldn't watch TV on the Sabbath and that everything would be shut.

As they unpacked in the room, a few features started to stand out. One bed had a double mattress on a single bed frame, with a base of two doors nailed together, one overlapping the other. The men tossed a coin to see who would have that unique experience. Mike ended up in the bed made of doors and during the night nearly went and joined Boxer in the Land Rover.

Boxer was more than happy to sleep in the vehicle, and it was added security for the small explosive devices they used for controlled detonation, but they often needed to open all the doors in the morning before entering.

Sunday morning arrived early, as the beds were as hard as stone, and the owners had left the plastic wrapping on the mattress, so every time you turned over you heard the soothing sound of crinkling plastic.

Boxer needed a morning walk, so they headed out to get the lay of the land. The islands could be quite beautiful in the early morning before the seemingly inevitable rain clouds arrived.

Mike and Dave thought they had been early risers, but somebody had already been out earlier, locking up all the kids' swings and slides. God forbid they had some fun on a Sunday.

Finding something to eat for lunch was going to prove interesting, but luckily there were some more Sassenachs in a mobile van selling burgers and chips to, it seemed, half the island's youth. Chatting with the locals, it seemed many outsiders were choosing to come here to escape the rat race, some attracted by the story of the forgotten island, which had only recently got modern conveniences, as they were often opposed by the island's unique sect of religious leaders. Too often, outsiders were greeted with scepticism towards their different ways, despite the considerable money they brought with them. The language barrier hadn't helped either, so they had formed their own small community.

That afternoon, Dave had planned to watch World Cup athletics on TV with the sound off, so as not to upset anybody, to pass the time and to see some of the distance races, but since the plug had been removed from the TV, that was going to be difficult, and, of course, the broadband was down, even though they had paid extra for it.

Feeling more than a little pissed off, the two men wandered through the town's long, narrow, grey streets. Colour, other than from nature, was notably absent, although the boats in the harbour were an exception. They continued to walk, hoping that maybe a pub or café might be open. No such luck, until they came across the local cinema, which seemed to have a café in the foyer, so they entered.

Jesus Christ Superhero the musical was playing, which seemed a bizarre choice for this island. Mike and Dave sat and ordered what turned out to be a rather good bacon butty and tea. As they ate, they started reading the local paper that had been left on the table. 'Blasphemy, Blasphemy' was the headline. This film screening had indeed caused quite a stir, and this was only the first night.

The two men tried to engage with the waitress and asked why this was such a big deal, as they ordered some more bacon butties. It hadn't caused any outcry, as far as they knew, anywhere else in the UK and was, in their understanding, a celebration of Jesus Christ. It was clear she wanted to say more, but she diplomatically stated, 'If you live on this sacred island for any period of time, you'll understand.'

Evidently, ministers lie down in front of car ferries to stop them running on the Sabbath!

There was even a rumour that Peter Dawson, the author who had made a name for himself as the leading voice against religion, had been seen arriving.

This really did seem to be a hard-core religion, quite a contrast to the chapel services Mike had regularly attended at school, which spoke of compassion, forgiveness and turning the other cheek. It was the one place during the busy school week he had felt calm and contemplative. He was never sure if it was the beautiful building that made him feel that way or the scripture. He did also love to sing.

Although they hadn't intended to see the film, their interest was now piqued, so they ate up and decided to come back later to see this compelling social experiment in action. Would the local paper's next headline be 'Outsider Who Runs Cinema Takes on Hard-Line Religious Zealots'? Probably not.

Upon returning to the cinema a couple of hours later, it was lit up like a scene from the nineteen forties and had some very odd vibes. There in front of them was a cordon of women in black coats and black headscarves, and a minister handing out leaflets. The two men took one and glanced at the main points; this was definitely the most interesting thing that had happened on the island for a while.

Reading the leaflet told them that, apparently, they were about to enter hell. Dave said it was not quite what he'd imagined, but he was willing to have his mind changed. This protest was adding to the entertainment value no end. They entered the cinema, bought two tickets, and walked towards the cinema doors. Another cordon had to be passed, another step closer to hell they were told, and their souls would be damned for ever if they took another step. They entered, got some sweets and took their seats.

It appeared the cordons were working, as only half a dozen people sat down for the screening. One cinema-goer rather spoiled the opening, as he fled from the cinema in tears, crying, 'I repent.'

As for the film itself, it seemed very upbeat and joyous, and Mike was sure if it had been about another religious leader, then those outside wouldn't be making such a fuss and might even enjoy watching it. Dave thought maybe not.

As they left, they were again cursed; their souls were now damned forever, and they would burn in hell. Some women even spat at their feet and, once clear of the cinema, stones were thrown at them. Dave wanted to go back and confront the perpetrators, but a night in the cells was going to screw the entire trip up, so they headed back, half laughing with incredulity. As a cinema experience, it had been memorable, hysterical and totally weird.

Returning to the guest house, they found the religious telegraph had been in action, and their room was now unfortunately double-booked for tomorrow, so they would have to move out. At this stage, a tent did seem like it would be just as comfortable.

Although pissed off, they were also in hysterics at the bizarre nature of what had happened; this was definitely hillbilly deliverance territory!

'Well, let's hope we're not cursed. Get the job done and get the hell out of this twilight zone,' said Mike.

In the morning, a new car battery was found and purchased. The young mechanic said a new alternator, maybe even a starter motor, was needed, but they didn't have one, so they would have to limit the use of the electrics.

He also said the cinema was now going to shut, due to some fire regulation violation they had conveniently found, which was 'bloody annoying, as it was about the only entertainment in the town for us youngsters.'

They left for the far side of the island, hoping they would get there before the tide closed the sea causeway.

Chapter 2

Although still very windy, the full ferocity of yesterday's storm had now passed over them. The sun was shining through the broken cloud. Campbell was outside the fishing lodge talking to the fly fishermen, who were eager to make their way out to the beats, having missed a day's fishing on the Saturday and Sunday being a no fishing day – almost unheard of at this time of year. One fisherman had been so insistent that something must be fishable on the Saturday that Campbell had taken him to the river to see the torrent of water cascading down the valley so he would realise it was almost impossible to see where the banks of rivers were, never mind to stand up and cast a fly. Beneath them, the pebble drive was pitted where the torrential rain had fallen, and seaweed was skirting the outside of the fishing lodge, having been ripped from the shoreline and scattered around.

Other than this, there seemed remarkably little damage, as most of the houses on the island were designed to survive winter storms. Though some roof tiles on a few outhouses would need replacing.

A Celtic carved stone pillar was also leaning on the ground; this was a favourite backdrop to many a fisherman's photograph showing off their catch. The ground beneath it had been battered by the wind tearing away the grass, and it was now leaning almost horizontally. Campbell went to lift it back up, shifting it a little before realising its enormous weight. He thought this was something his associate Finn would like to demonstrate his strength by lifting.

It was still before seven in the morning, yet the river had fallen dramatically on the Sunday as only a spate river feed by lochs can, all the fishermen were already set up eager for the nine o'clock start. Although they'd lost a day's fishing, the rain was what they'd desperately hoped for so the salmon could enter the river after the recent drought. They'd had several days where barely a fish had been caught, whatever type of fly or method had been tried, and it was frustrating to return each night to their accommodation and see that the sea loch in front of them was teeming with thousands of salmon. The shoals boiling on the surface every ten minutes with their dorsal fins breaking through as they desperately waited for there to be enough water to enter the Gumerston river system teased the frustrated onlookers.

Several of the fishermen were lobbying Colonel Bentley – as chairman of the fishing syndicate – to let them start early, since they'd missed a day. But he was holding fast, reminding them all of the rules they had willing agreed to but were now trying to break: to start not one minute before nine and to finish bang on five in the evening.

Campbell had let the ghillies finish their breakfast a little early, and they had loaded the estate minibus with all the fishing gear, clipping the almost twenty rods to a slightly rusting roof rack with a rather frayed bungee cord. The minibus was full and getting a bit steamed up as they waited for the driver. There were a number of frustrated murmurs of disquiet prior to Pete emerging and opening the driver's door. Several of the ghillies expected Pete to be taken to task, but not a word was said. Was it the fact Pete's face was scarred like a broken bottle, or had his rumoured reputation for having a short temper even extended to the fishing guests?

By the time the minibus departed from the front of the lodge, Finn had already challenged some of Campbell's special operational staff to see if they could lift the Celtic pillar stone back to its vertical position. The three men, who were mainly dressed in black with cropped hair and military tattoos, each took a turn. All but one failed, and that man put the stone down almost as soon as he'd lifted it. Finn then reached down, lifted the stone, and planted it back in its standing position as others placed stones around the base to secure it and topped it off with the grass that had so recently been torn away. It was another show of dominant strength from the Russian in front of these specialist contractors.

As the breakfast was being cleared and the dishes were being done, Annie watched Finn through the window as he lifted the stone with a deep sigh as well as some frustration that the housekeeper didn't seem to want to replace the broken dishwasher, which would make her life much easier.

When the dishes were dried and put away, Annie asked the cook, 'Is it Yana that's locked in the larder?'

The cook replied in a serious, resigned tone, 'Don't ask, Child. Questions get you in trouble. Just get on with your job, if you know what's good for you.'

The housekeeper entered Campbell's office to be asked, 'Have you done a thorough unpacking of all the new guests? Anything to report?'

'Mr Phillips turned out to be a journalist. Looks like he's paying for the ex-defence minister's trip to get an in-depth scoop on the scandal that made him resign, but Munro has given him nothing new so far, and his notepads suggest he's getting fairly pissed off.'

'Keep an eye on the notepads; they may give us something useful. Anything new on Earl Hunberry?' asked Campbell.

'He seems to have commissioned a whole photoshoot to put into a magazine of very large women wearing fishing waders, bound up with fishing line, with fishing flies through their nipples. Seems quite proud of it and has shown it around, but he doesn't seem to have any takers for it so far.'

'His pal, Lord Helmsworth?'

Seems nice enough, but my god, how on earth did they make him head of that bird association? The ghillies were asking him to name some birds, which he kept getting wrong, so when a heron flew over they told him it was a vulture, and now he wants to write a piece in the association magazine about the furthest northern sighting of a vulture and that it's a sign of global warming!'

'Next!' said Campbell.

'Just the headmaster of that famous boarding school in London. He's paying for the whole beat himself, so not short of money. Perfectly manicured nails for a man and has a collection of about a dozen different canes for, I presume, beating the boys at his school, but why he has them here, god knows. Strikes me he could be really nasty; I wouldn't be surprised to see him in a Sunday newspaper exposé.'

'What about the prince next week? I know he's important, but is he one of your special guests too?' the housekeeper then asked.

'Just helping him out over a particular problem; got to do your bit for the royals, you know.'

At that moment, a rifle shot rang out, giving them both a bit of a jolt.

'Bloody Calum again, trying to blow up that sea mine in the estuary. They must have fired a couple of hundred rounds at it yesterday, trying to hit one of the prongs and blow it sky high, before I told them to stop wasting ammo. Tell him to stop when you leave, please.'

'Just a couple of things left. Prince John to get Colonel Bentley's room? Yes? His pilot in the end annex? Colonel Bentley in the room beside the wine cellar, or is that too tempting?'

'All sounds good,' replied Campbell.

'The larder seems to be full. It's never good here when the larder is full – too many questions. Can you sort it quickly, please?'

'Duly noted,' replied Campbell, as another high-powered round sent shock waves through the air.

'Yes, I'll go and sort that little bugger out,' said the housekeeper as she left the office, nearly walking into Finn, who was entering.

'I saw you showing off to the kids that you still have it,' said Campbell as he entered the room.

'I'm not sure those battle-hardened bastards would like to be called kids,' said Finn.

'When you get past sixty, you all look so damn young.'

'What about our cargo? It's been delayed three days. The factory ship has followed the fish into the sea estuary, so it's not too far away. Is the coble boat big enough to shift the load, or do we wait for one of the trawlers to get back from Oban?' asked Finn.

'If we get the fly fishers on the lochs with their rowing boats, I think we can use the coble boat. Even if we delay loading some of the bales till next week, we need to get the black packages picked up. Send Kristijonas – he knows what he's doing – plus a couple of the young lads to help him. Ask Pete when he returns from dropping the fishers off if the ghillies managed to get the rowing boats out okay. If they did, green-light for Kristijonas.

As each group of fishers was dropped by their beats, they quickly shuffled off in anticipation of an exciting day. Lord Helmsworth was poised at the Laird's Cast, the first main fishing pool on the first beat, which was nearest the sea estuary. He had set up his carbon fishing rod with a sink tip and a shrimp fly and was in visibly heightened anticipation of a fish taking at any moment, as he seemed to alternate from slow, careful casting, which the wind kept blowing out of position, to faster, more powerful casts that splashed into the water, startling any fish close by. He kept checking his fly hadn't been lost or become knotted due to the wind. The river, although still high, had dropped dramatically from the day before. The light was good, and this was maybe the best place in the whole river system, and yet nothing was taking. His ghillie could see the mounting frustration cascading over him.

'Just go and fish it again. Try a silver stoat's tail because of the peaty water,' encouraged Cameron.

Lord Helmsworth started again at the top of the pool, covering the water with careful casting. Nothing happened. Had all the salmon run through to the other beats? As the ghillie looked towards the bottom of the pool, there appeared to be a large ripple coming out of nowhere. It was a huge surge of salmon creating a bow wave in front of them.

It all happened in about ten minutes. There were hundreds, maybe thousands of fish entering the pool. All you could see were dorsal fins breaking the surface as they swiftly moved through. As they got to the narrower head of the pool, many salmon were beaching themselves on the riverbank in their mad rush to get up the river; tens of silver bars were thrashing about trying to re-enter the water. By this time, Lord Helmsworth had dropped his rod and was kicking the salmon up the bank. He wasn't going to let this opportunity pass him by. His ghillie, however, was doing the opposite, throwing the stranded fish back into the river. Lord Helmsworth shouted at him, 'What the hell are you doing?'

The ghillie pointed to the cars that had just stopped to see this rare natural phenomenon in action, and suggested that maybe this was not the most sporting of ways to catch salmon.

Lord Helmsworth looked at the three salmon he'd kicked behind the fishing hut, which was shielded from view, and like a dog that had stolen something juicy, he guarded them before promptly hitting them over the head with his priest and using his fishing fly to tear the flesh on the edge of their mouths to make it look like they were caught fairly.

After that extraordinary morning, the rest of the day's catch was rather disappointing. There were salmon everywhere, but all they had on their minds after weeks of waiting for enough water to enter the river was to keep running upwards and onwards towards the spawning grounds. Lord Helmsworth only added another two salmon to the day's catch, which turned out to be more than most of the other beats by about two fish.

As per Campbell's instructions back at the lodge, Finn, having got the okay from Pete about the ghillies being able to launch their rowing boats, dispatched Kristijonas with a couple of young helpers to the ageing but solid blue-and-white-painted coble boat with its slow but reliable diesel engine, which they had just filled up and launched from the boathouse and had anchored by the jetty in front of the lodge in anticipation of leaving. Finn threw in some very old-looking lifejackets, and they departed to retrieve the cargo.

As they cast off, Finn walked back to the lodge to deal with the problem locked up in the larder. Yana was still rather damp, having been dragged from the side of a peat bank in the early hours of the morning in her vain attempt to escape Campbell's clutches. When they apprehended her, she was soaked to the skin. They had thrown her into the larder and locked her up. Unfortunately for her, she'd made her attempt to flee during one of the worst storms in living memory. The larder she was held in was almost as cold as she was, but it had a basic bed with a couple of sheets, and she used one to dry herself off and the other to keep herself from freezing.

Finn opened the door, holding what looked like a charred lump of flesh in his hand. She could tell from his look that any questions were going to come later, after a severe beating. She instinctively turned away from him, and as she did, he hit her in the back with a crushing blow. She let out a primal howl that seemed to last forever and dragged herself to the corner of the room. Finn, not a novice to inflicting pain, was himself taken aback. Had he broken her spine or ruptured a vital organ? She was clearly in agony. He assessed that another blow may damage her irrevocably, rendering her unable to give them the information they needed. He stopped, looked at her cowering, half-naked body in the corner of the room and said, 'I will return later, and you will tell me everything.' As he left, he wondered if she would be still alive when he came back.

Finn was convinced that Yana had been sent by Viktor, the owner of the nightclub in Moscow she'd worked at and the fixer who arranged many of the special packages that arrived at regular intervals at the fishing lodge. So, on his return, when Finn led with 'Did Viktor send you to spy on us?' Yana sighed deep inside. This she could spin, to confirm his conclusion with just enough information to make it believable, that that was why she'd accessed Campbell's laptop, to check the percentage Viktor was receiving was correct.

Finn would relay her explanation to Campbell before her fate could be decided. Campbell had a reputation for thoroughness that was well deserved, and he would wait for his source in Moscow to confirm or deny this story.

When Finn entered Campbell's office to update him, Campbell had Cameron the head ghillie with him. Campbell had just asked him to look after Prince John the following week. Cameron asked if there was anything he should know. He'd heard from another ghillie on the Dee that the prince liked to make a drama out of every fish, and that he often strayed on to other beats without permission and hated anybody catching more fish than him.

Campbell replied, 'Cameron, you dealt with Johnson last week – this will be a breeze.'

Chapter 3

The Russian factory ship was enormous, grey, ominous and the size of a cruise liner. The front was folded down like the jaw of a giant robot. It was in full operation. And parked five hundred yards off the Scottish coast, in full violation of international laws. Finlay had seen one before at sea, but seen against the houses that dotted the sea loch it revealed its true enormous size, like an industrial factory sucking up every fish in the sea.

The local fishermen had been feasting on a bonanza of herring, which the recent storm had pushed into the sea loch. They had filled their legal quotas for landing the catch ashore and were now filling up the Russian ship like bees bringing nectar to a hive.

The Russian sailors had taken this chance to go ashore and buy Scottish cigarettes and whiskey. The chances of a fishery patrol vessel arriving on the scene were next to nil, as they were all tied up in the English Channel playing politics.

One twenty-foot coble fishing boat, with lobster creels on deck, was rowing the last few metres into the mouth of this vast behemoth, like a gnat entering a fish's jaw. It wasn't there for the fishing.

A shout came from the boat. 'Tell Aleksei it's Kristijonas. We have some packages to pick up.'

Aleksei appeared a few minutes later, a large, rugged man with a chin curtain of a beard. He beckoned Kristijonas to him, pointing at two large packages, and imparted some detailed instructions. Kristijonas nodded.

A number of boxes and bags arrived. Each was carefully checked off and put in the small hold in the bow of the coble with the greatest of care.

Kristijonas was always curious to try to find out what had arrived, but mostly he was in the dark. Was it a German expressionist painting supposedly destroyed by the Nazis or some museum pieces from Dresden? Sometimes it was a passenger.

Kristijonas didn't ask too many questions – that resulted in pain and, once stung, was not to be repeated. But Kristijonas knew the packages were destined for those who came to the exclusive, members-only fishing estate that was spoken of in hallowed terms as having the best fishing in the world. Most of the anglers simply came to fish for salmon, but a select few left with packages that were paid for in influence, votes, real estate and much more. Mainly these obligations happened in the UK and its offshore banking territories, but sometimes across the world. One lord who was renowned for loving exclusive items from the Third Reich left wearing Himmler's Nazi uniform, but most were silent and opaque about their dealings.

The journey back to the fishing lodge was only about fifteen miles from where the factory ship was busily filling up its hold with herring. The weather conditions were clear but gusty, with choppy waves. The ferocious storm that had driven the fish inshore, and the factory ship to follow, had abated, and the sun was breaking through.

The small, wooden coble boat was solid but slow, and as the waves started to get bigger, Kristijonas turned the boat towards them to stop the waves from crashing over the side and drenching them. Kristijonas, who rarely bothered wearing a life jacket, glanced at the bow of the boat to see if the jackets were in a fit state if needed; they were. He changed the direction of the boat as they zigged and zagged across the most open part of the route home.

They were making good progress despite the choppy waves and were only a few miles from home. Kristijonas asked Finlay to bale some water out of the boat, then looked ahead and saw what looked like a ghostly spiral. Almost invisible, it seemed to be gripping the surface of the water and drawing it up. It had him transfixed. Was it a tornado? He'd seen them in clips from America but had never seen one here. He asked Angus, who was an islander, if he'd seen anything like it before. Angus said no, but there was folklore about them. Kristijonas took out his phone to video it, as no one would believe him otherwise. He then almost lost hold of his phone as the boat rocked. He looked at the sea beside him, which had started to pull up. It had gone from choppy to biblical in seconds. A sea tornado had hit them!

The wind change was ferocious. In a heartbeat, the boat was being pushed and pulled around. Kristijonas went to the motor to increase the power, but the engine started to rev and the boat was hardly moving at all. Was the engine in gear? Was there something stuck around the propeller? What was going on? They needed to get the hell out of there quick. The boat was heading for some huge, jagged rocks with a sea cliff beyond. 'It's the wind; it's the wind; it's creating so much air around the boat, the propeller has little to grip on!' Kristijonas held the tiller in position and shouted, 'Grab an oar. We're going to have to row!'

The wind had drawn the seawater up so they were now inside a wall of rain. They could barely see each other, and the water was beating down on their faces like hail. They needed to row for the other shore, which was about four hundred yards away, or get smashed to pieces. Finlay and Angus took one oar each and rowed as hard as possible. At least the oars were giving them some purchase, and they were moving. The wooden oars were flexing, creaking, bending as they rowed for their lives. They could barely see where they were going but were slowly pulling away. Kristijonas was trying to hold the tiller straight while bailing water and wishing he had a powerful outboard motor rather than this feeble diesel.

So much water was coming on board … so much. They needed to bail for their lives. Kristijonas tied the tiller in place as best he could and bailed.

'I can't see a fucking thing,' said Finlay.

'Keep calm, row and bail, row and bail.'

'It's fucking surreal, being caught in the middle of this hell.'

Angus shouted, 'I have nothing left. I really need to swap over. I have nothing left. Nothing.'

'Have you got hold of the oar, Finlay? Are you sure? We can't lose one or we're dead,' said Kristijonas as he took over from Angus and started rowing. So much water was on board. Angus was throwing bucketloads overboard, but they were still ankle deep.

'Just bail, just bail, we're not going down without a fight.'

Bang. They hit something. Was it the shore? Was it a rock?

'I still can't see a bloody thing,' said Angus.

'Swap again!' shouted Finlay. He had both oars now, as he'd taken the one from Kristijonas.

Crack. The oar blade broke. They hadn't loaded a spare oar. Shit. Nothing to do now but grab a life jacket and hold on to the boat.

The boat tossed and turned, despite the weight of water in it, and the wooden hull started to split where it had just hit the rocks. Kristijonas had his life jacket on now and decided to jump. Hitting the water with a splash, he sank. There was no buoyancy! He seemed to fall through the water like it was froth, then suddenly he was flung up and onto the surface. He coughed out some water and swam for the rock they had just hit.

The maelstrom moved away a hundred yards, then two. Around him, it was sunny with blue skies as the cauldron of wind and rain left. Really quite beautiful, in a bizarre way.

The boat had disappeared. Sunk. Kristijonas gripped the slippery, wet rock for all he was worth. He was reluctant to slacken his grip, even though he could see the storm was moving well away. In the distance, he could see a magenta life jacket moving slowly towards him. Was it Finlay or Angus? He scanned around him again but could see just one person swimming in his direction.

Kristijonas felt so lucky to have survived and was momentarily engulfed by a wave of euphoria before a sudden feeling of gut-wrenching dread took its place. Campbell would kill him for losing the cargo.

Chapter 4

Julian Campbell sat in his rather battered Eames lounge chair looking across the sea estuary from his office, contemplating the events that had brought him to this point in his life. He was the driver of this dual operation, importing items almost impossible to get into this country, under the cover of being head gamekeeper, on this exclusive and prestigious sporting estate during the fishing season and from his London townhouse in the winter months.

This fit was working very well, with easy access to artefacts coming in from Russia as well as the more mundane white powder. He had access to some of the most influential members of the British establishment and some from across the world.

Julian Campbell was ex-MI6 and in his sixties. He looked worn from the world he existed in but was always well dressed, in hand-tailored clothing that had become threadbare in places. Looking into his eyes, they were cold, calculating. He also had a leg missing. How it had happened was never clear, but it had happened in Berlin before the wall fell.

Campbell had little sense of personal space, and when you talked to him he seemed to get closer and closer until he seemed to be breathing your air, but no one was brave enough to object. It was like encountering a particularly venomous snake; just getting away without harm or compromise was a result. He also used his disability to cling to young men he liked; as they helped him in and out of cars or boats, he would linger. He was like a virus that needed to be socially distanced.

In his other role as head gamekeeper he could also act as a great host, showing enthusiastic interest in the day's catches and being very pleasant company. It was as if he'd played two different people all his life.

Campbell had uncovered the small network of smugglers using fishing boats when, as an MI6 boss, he was hunting down the supply routes used by the IRA. It had been assumed to be very unlikely that there were Scots supplying arms and explosives to the struggle, but they had underestimated these islanders, who through some twisted logic even hated the mainland Scots, as they didn't speak Gaelic. They also despised the English, even though most had never met one, and they were even undecided about the islanders from Skye, particularly when the bridge to the mainland was opened. They also thought they were the chosen people and therefore deserved more – a fatal combination.

The idea of border controls or being intercepted by a naval vessel did not, in practice, exist north of the Isle of Skye. Supplying the IRA had offered vast rewards, and buying arms and explosives from the Russian trawlers worked for both the Russians and Americans in support of the struggle. The islanders, having drunk from that poisoned chalice, found this would not be a short-term contract.

When Campbell and his spooks had caught up with those few boats supplying the IRA, he gave them a choice: work for him, so he knew what arms were going where, or face life in prison. It was a simple decision.

When the Good Friday agreement was signed, Campbell left MI6 and hatched a plan to get rich and be a man of influence in Britain, using the same few fishing boats to bring in items that couldn't easily be secured elsewhere.

The Kremlin were more than happy to oblige, through his Cold War Russian KGB contacts. As the EU expanded, and the UK in particular welcomed in former Soviet countries, the Russian leader knew he needed to push back against Britain in particular, before the call to freedom arrived too close to home.

One boat crew who thought they'd done their bit and weren't up for this new arrangement were mysteriously lost with all hands at sea. The other two boat crews fell in line, happy to continue being generously paid and to have lavish houses and cars in their island villages.

Campbell had two right-hand men. One was Pete, who had a disfigured face – we were told from a car crash, but who knew the real reason? He was not somebody you wanted to meet on a dark night and could be very volatile but extremely loyal. The other, Finn, had two jobs: to be close to Campbell but also to report directly to his Russian handlers, who were supplying the drugs and the articles of influence via the Russian fish factory ships.

Finn's Russian name was Avimelekh, which no islander could pronounce properly. One day his name changed, when he came back with a fin of a pilot whale. He had been driving along the coastal road and had seen this pod of four whales stranded on a mud bank several miles down the estuary. As others were arriving to try to get them back in the water, he waded up through the thick mud to the biggest whale, climbed on top of it and cut its dorsal fin clean off as its exhausted body tried in vain to throw him off. The name Finn stuck, along with its ominous association, which he enjoyed. He stuck the fin on the mantelpiece in the staff side of the lodge. The smell alone was a powerful reminder.

Five miles away, back on the sea rock, Kristijonas had waited for Finlay to swim to him, still shaken up by what had just happened, and then together they swam the hundred yards to the shore.

They walked the peninsula shoreline, looking for Angus, but could see no sign of him. As they searched and walked, they were getting colder and colder, so they decided to go back to the lodge for help.

As they approached, they were both shivering, half through the cold, half through fear of what lay ahead.

When they entered the large, wooden-floored meeting room with its whiff of wet raincoats and rubber waders drying, the ghillies had finished their day's toil and were either sitting in the sagging armchairs and sofas drinking bottled beer or playing pool. Finn was sitting at a table at the far end chatting to Pete, who had just returned to the fishing estate after serving a two-month prison stretch after getting into a bar fight in Glasgow at New Year over some football match he didn't really care too much about.

As Kristijonas entered the room and slowly walked down it to speak to Finn, everybody could see from his face that something very serious had occurred. As he reached Finn and began his whispered explanation, Finn's face seemed to lose all expression. A frost quickly spread across the room, people's voices quietened and eyes moved away from Finn, Pete and Kristijonas to the floor. A couple of people looked to see if they had time to slip away and then thought better of it. Then, in an instant, Pete picked up a snooker ball in his fist and planted it in Kristijonas face several times. Kristijonas crumpled to the floor and was unconscious in seconds, lying in an expanding pool of his own blood.

Finn ordered, 'Everybody get their kit back on. It's going to be a long night.'

Finn and Campbell planned the search: get the launch out, walk the shoreline, get one of the trawlers back to use its sonar. They needed to find this boat, and fast.

'Pete, if you do something like that again without my say-so, you're gone,' Campbell warned. 'Get Kristijonas in. I need to speak to him.'

Chapter 5

The morning was wet and blowy as Mike and Dave drove towards the fishing lodge. They had phoned ahead to the head gamekeeper, a man called Campbell, who seemed to be a little surprised they were coming. Mike explained Colonel Bentley had contacted Naval Command for them to clear the mine before Prince John arrived.

The Gumerston fishing lodge was on a smaller island peninsula to the far west of Tumelray. It was about twenty miles by fifteen in size and could be crossed over to by a causeway, which the tide covered for several hours a day, making it unpassable. There was a small village about five miles away, and a few croft houses were dotted around, some of which had become derelict.

As they drove towards the half-mile-long causeway, the tide was rising, but only up to tyre level, so it was okay for the Land Rover to cross. The island stood as if cracked away from the main island, with towering cliffs and colonies of soaring seabirds. It looked ominous, with water cascading over the cliff face in places like a scene from a Tolkien novel. The lodge was another five miles away, over a hill and along a coastal road. The fishing lodge appeared in the distance as they got over the first hill – a large, whitewashed old building. As they got closer, they could see it had a few turrets and was sitting on the edge of the sea estuary. To the rear of the lodge were a couple of dozen mature trees with walls surrounding them, a welcome patch of green on the otherwise barren, brown, treeless island. There were also a few outhouses to the back of it.

Finn greeted them – a Russian in the Outer Hebrides! They chatted briefly to get a location on the mine and to enquire how a Russian had ended up here, to which they got little insight. They looked to see the best place to launch the boat from, the jetty in front of the lodge being ideal.

They quickly got the impression they were wanted in and out of here as fast as possible.

Mike reversed the Land Rover down the jetty to launch the RIB (rigid inflatable boat, just like many lifeboat crews use). Getting it into the water with ease, Dave tied the RIB up, and both got changed into their wetsuits. Mike then loaded the remaining equipment, and Dave triple-checked everything, as was his way. They launched the RIB into the sea estuary and headed for the last reported sighting.

Boxer stayed with the Land Rover as a security measure, although she always wanted to come with them.

The mine had been bobbing around in the estuary for a few days, moving in and out with the tides and wind, and as there was at present barely a breeze, the calmer water would make it fairly easy to find. They made a grid search in the boat heading towards the river mouth and quickly found the mine a few hundred yards up from the fishing lodge. As they'd thought when they'd seen Toby's photo, it was most likely a Second World War moored mine that had been drifting for many years but was still very dangerous. As they came close, they could see it was rusty after many decades at sea but in remarkable condition considering, with contact horns ready to go *boom*!

On closer examination, the mine had several recent indentations on its surface. It looked like someone, maybe the gamekeeper, had tried to blow it up by firing bullets at it, hoping for a grand explosion, but this was extremely difficult to do at any distance.

As they started the process of assessment, they could see they were being observed by a few people. Just curiosity, they concluded.

Dave launched the Sea Fox UAV (underwater autonomous vehicle) to check if this was a lone mine or whether there was a string, with others submerged. This UAV was a new, smaller, more manoeuvrable version to those used on minesweepers, but nearly as effective, with sonar, cameras and infrared all linked back to a laptop. This made the entire process less brutal, crude and up close. Thankfully, it was only one mine with a chain attached. Dave loved his new toy and was trying a range of different approaches and sensors to see what gave the most complete picture.

They deployed their homemade catch mechanism, which had proved a very effective device for retrieval, so they could manoeuvre the mine into position for EOD (Explosive Ordnance Disposal).

The mine was now secured, and the horns were covered with specialist caps. The detonator now needed removing.

Dave carefully, quietly and methodically started to remove the rust to see if a wrench could be used to unscrew the fitting or whether it would need to be quietly drilled out. Forty minutes and many silent curses later, the detonator finally came out, and the mine was safe.

They unpacked the TNT explosive from the mine and piled it into a heap on the shore, ready to be burnt. Once ignited, it fizzled and spat like a large dud firework. The detonator was dealt with separately and blown up in a small controlled explosion.

Job done, time to head home.

As they approached the fishing lodge, they could again see a number of silhouettes on the hillside. As they backed the Land Rover and trailer into the water to pick up the RIB and secure it, they saw an ex-military patrol boat approaching, which docked on the other side of the jetty with what looked like ex-military personnel on board. They thought this seemed a little over the top for a fishing lodge on the fringes of Scotland.

They gathered all their kit together and let Boxer out to run along the shore for a few minutes to let off steam and do her business.

Finn emerged, so they gave him a quick debrief and then asked, 'What's with the patrol boat?'

'Oh, we have lots of poachers here. It works as a deterrent.'

Mike whistled to Boxer, and as she approached Finn, she gave out a very low, burbling growl.

'Bad Boxer,' Mike said. 'Sorry, she never really growls.'

Finn asked, 'What is the torpedo thing?'

Dave started to explain in detail, but Mike cut in; he knew Dave's explanation could go on a long time, and he wanted to see if they could make it back to the mainland that day. They said goodbye and drove off.

'That was weird,' said Mike. 'That one person in a thousand that dogs instinctively don't like.'

Chapter 6

'Well, Dave, that went rather bloody well. Those curses don't seem to have worked after all.'

'You mean, apart from the forty minutes it took to release the casing that was solid with rust?'

Dave was growing more and more impressed with the new AUV. Everything was so clear; the graphs and readouts showed so much detail, everything clear as a bell. Some of those shoals of salmon were huge, and the seals chasing them around, even old tin cans, were all showing up and easily identified. Ruddy awesome.

'When I started in this business, you felt around in the dark, hugging the mine and hoping the bubbles from your tank didn't set it off.'

'God, those guys were weird. Just not buying that anti-poaching story.'

'Yes, there's some serious ex-military there.'

'Fancy stopping for a drink?'

'God, it's a bit early for me.'

'Check the ferry. See if we can get off this godforsaken island today.'

'No, we'll have to wait until Wednesday. Crap.'

'Tent tonight, or try to find another outstanding B&B?'

'Tent, yes.'

'Since we're here now, how about going to see those standing stones? They say they're better than Stonehenge.'

'I'll believe that when I see it. I was a bit disappointed with Stonehenge. It looks bigger on the TV.'

'Pop it in the sat-nav, see if it's close.'

'Four miles. Let's go see them.'

'We have a few brews in the back, unless Boxer's been at them. Remember that time she broke into the fridge and chewed into a couple of cans? Not sure if that was pee or beer we cleared up, and what a hangover she had.'

'Didn't do it again, though, did she?'

'Wow, not quite as big as Stonehenge, but more standing stones, and what a view out to sea!'

'Crack open the beers and grab that supermarket cooked chicken.'

They sat at the end of the standing stones, watching the sun and broken cloud play with the shadows on the stones as they drank the beer and ate the chicken, throwing bits to Boxer.

'Do you think we can pitch the tent near here, or are the locals going to go mental – "sacred site" and all?'

'We can go back to that mini mart at the petrol station and see if they can give us a steer. Get some snacks too.'

'Let's book that ferry for tomorrow. I don't want to be here any longer than we have to. There might be a decent mobile signal near the petrol station, or even a landline.'

'No, you can't camp at the stone circle,' they were told. Snacks bought, Mike used the landline to book the ferry.

Just as they finished paying, two of the men they'd seen at the lodge came into the shop. 'Hi guys, we need to talk',

'Not another mine, I hope.'

'No, we need you to come back.'

'Sorry mate, not going to happen. We're booked to the mainland tomorrow.'

'We'll make it well worth your time, double your normal fee. We need you to find a boat.'

'That could take days, maybe weeks. Contact the coastguard.'

'You have the remote-controlled submarine that could find it for us.'

'MoD equipment isn't for civilian use; plus, we have other jobs. An unexploded missile in a Caithness loch needs our attention.'

One of the men opened his jacket to reveal a pistol, then the other man did the same. 'You will come with us.'

Dave, calm as you like, asked, 'You want a fight here? Let's go for it in front of everybody in the whole fucking shop. Is that what your boss wants?'

The two men backed off a little. Mike and Dave started walking the hundred yards back to the Land Rover, wishing they'd parked a bit closer.

They could hear footsteps behind them. Were the men just going to pull their guns on them as they got into the Land Rover?

Mike put his hand in his pocket, feeling for a silent whistle. He put it to his lips and blew. No response. Was Boxer sodding asleep? The men from the lodge were getting closer. Mike and Dave tried to walk quicker, but casually. Mike saw Dave's fist start to clench.

Crash, thud, Boxer was charging towards the men, fearless, barking and growling at them. Everybody was looking in their direction. The two men from the lodge moved slowly back to their grey van, crisis over.

Dave started the Land Rover, driving off quickly. Mike observed one of the two men in the grey van on a walkie-talkie.

'We need to get clear of here and go to the main town. The more people, the better. They might even have police.'

Dave nodded in agreement.

'What's going on with these guys? Guns in their jackets? Was that for real or just for effect?'

'Looked real to me,' came Dave's reply.

'Let's put our foot down. Get off these single-track roads as soon as possible.'

'Where are they? Behind us?'

'Can't see them. Keep going, get across that causeway.'

'Are they following?'

'Nothing right behind us yet. What height's the tide at? Can we cross yet?'

They passed a small quarry, and as they did, they could see a tractor coming towards them. They slowed and pulled into a passing place to let it go by. As the tractor approached, it paused in front of them, then drove straight at them, making contact and pushing the Land Rover off the road and into the ditch.

'Dickhead islander. What the hell is he doing? Are you okay? Is Boxer okay?'

'What a bloody arsehole.'

Dave grabbed at the door to confront the moron of a tractor driver and saw an AK-47 machine gun pointing straight at him. 'Fucking ambush.'

The van from the lodge pulled up behind them. The two men got out, pistols in hand, accompanied by a young, aggressive Doberman.

The back of the Land Rover had swung open during the crash. Mike told Boxer to stay where she was. The Doberman was getting closer to the Land Rover and was becoming more aggressive. Boxer flew out of the rear door, chasing after the Doberman, jumping on its back. Boxer's teeth sank into the Doberman's neck. With blood pouring out, the Doberman was squealing, yelping and running away. Boxer came back to the Land Rover, saw Pete was pulling at Mike and attacked him, ripping at his arm.

One of the men lifted his pistol and fired at Boxer, just missing both of them, much to Pete's fury at being nearly shot. Mike then shouted 'Away, away' to Boxer, who backed off to a safe distance. The Doberman came back, got viciously kicked by Finn and also got a gun-butt blow to the head from Pete.

A car was approaching in the far distance, on the coastal road. With the machine gun still pointed at them, Dave and Mike were quickly ushered out of the Land Rover and pushed into the back of the grey van. Cable ties were bound around their hands and feet.

Their RIB was unlatched from the Land Rover and put onto the tow bar of the van.

'What the hell are you guys doing? We work for the Naval Command; there are going to be people looking for us.'

'You said you were private contractors.'

'They're still going to miss us.'

Finn's response was a right and left hook to Dave and Mike, who then shared a long look. What would be their next move? How were they going to get out of this?

The grey van then moved off, with the boat and mini-sub attached.

Boxer was running behind, following the van. The Doberman was limping and staying put.

Pete shouted to Finn, 'I'm going to shoot that fucking dog! It ruined my jacket!' His arm was seeping with blood.

'Don't hit the fucking boat, or you're dead,' was Finns reply.

Pete opened one of the van's back doors to get a clear shot. He fired. The first shot missed. Almost instinctively, Boxer moved behind the boat for cover, but as the van slowed for a corner, Boxer came into clear view of Pete's pistol, and he raised it to fire again.

Without thinking, Mike threw himself towards Pete. They both fell out of the moving van, bouncing off the rubber bow of the boat. Mike had landed on top of Pete, breaking his fall somewhat. He rolled down the road banking. The cable ties on his feet had broken during the fall.

Mike started to run like hell across the moor, with Boxer following. He stumbled on a sticky bit of bog, looked around and saw no cover, just peat, bog and heather. Nobody was following him yet.

He stopped to wrestle free of the cable ties on his hands, using a rough rock to abrade the fixing point.

A car stopped behind the van, and a tourist got out to help Pete, who was still lying on the tarmac.

Crouching over him, the tourist asked, 'Anything broken'?

'No, I'm alright. Now piss off.'

'Okay, just trying to help.'

Dave was pushed to the floor of the van with a gun in his back, so he was out of sight of the tourist's car.

That had given Mike vital time to get some distance between himself and the van.

The grey van moved to the next layby to let the tourist's car go by.

'Get that guy back,' shouted Finn.

Pete and one of the other men could see Mike a couple of hundred yards away, and they started the chase across the moor, which was wet through after recent rain – not the easiest terrain to cover fast, even when dry.

The first bullet that passed Mike seemed surreal. Was that an actual bullet that had hit the rock in front of him? Mike hadn't heard the shot but was running so hard he may have blocked it out. The second was no mistake; a clump of peat moor tore up by his left foot as a blast from a high-powered rifle rang out across the moor.

Mike was now running flat-out, telling himself keep loose, knees high, or you're going to trip on the heather underfoot, just like he'd done whilst doing the Caledonian Run with Dave. Weave from side to side as much as possible to make it harder to be hit, and just go.

Mike was gaining distance when he saw it: a stream, or as the Scots call it, a burn, cut deep through the heather and about twelve feet across. Was it jumpable? If he went down, could he get back up quickly enough, without being a sitting duck on the other side? Boxer was just ahead of him. He felt he had no choice. If he jumped and missed, at least he could hit the other side and pull himself up by the heather. Right, Boxer, the jump of our life coming up! Mike had the speed with him. Here goes … shit … something caught his foot. *Crash. Wallop.*

What the hell had had he landed in? A stream? It should have a hard gravel bottom, but this was soft as shit. Bugger, he was sinking, going down fast, thighs disappearing. It was now up to his waist.

Mike desperately grabbed at the heather to stop himself from sinking deeper. He tried to pull himself up with it, but the heather gave way. Shit, it was strong enough to stop him sinking any further but not strong enough to get him out. Mike tried again, this time putting as much even pressure on the heather roots as he could so he didn't jerk them out.

There was so much suction holding him down that the heather roots broke again.

Boxer was trying to get down to Mike, but the banking was steep, giving her little grip. Mike put out a hand to grab Boxer. Between them, he could stay put and not sink any further.

Pete arrived.

'You dickhead. I'm going to shoot you full of sodding holes, and that bloody dog too.'

He shot at Boxer and just grazed the top of her shoulder. 'Go away, go away,' Mike shouted. Boxer retreated, half growling, half whimpering.

Pete took aim directly at him raising the gun slowly, then bringing the gun down and then back up, finger on the trigger. Mike took a deep breath. Pete fired. The bullet missed Mike, but Pete was laughing, clearly enjoying the moment. He raised the gun again, then stopped and turned.

Finn had arrived, and Pete turned to him and said, 'This arsehole is going to die. We don't need him. The other one is the operator of the sub.'

Finn nodded. 'Okay, but we don't shoot him.'

'What, are you fecking kidding me?'

Finn looked at Mike, who was sinking deeper. 'He is not getting out of there alive – just another tourist dying in the wilderness. No bullets, no police, just an accident.'

'Fuck, I want to kill him.'

Pete turned and threw a rock at Mike in disgust and then fired a shot into the air.

Finn, 'Okay, back to the van. Let's see what Campbell says.'

Chapter 7

I suppose it could be worse, thought Mike. I could be dead. He was now up to his armpits in a mixture of mud, peat and silt, and left to die in the middle of a remote moor. What the hell? What the hell, indeed.

Come on, assess the situation; you're an engineer, think it out. Feck, who put this death trap in the middle of a pissing Scottish moor? Why is it in a stream? Weird! Does it matter? Not one sodding bit.

Mike looked around. He could only reach one side of the gully, and the side he could reach, he had already pulled most of the heather roots out of. The remaining clump was keeping him from sinking further. He could see some pebbles further downstream, but as he pressed with his free hand, he could find nothing solid. The stream was shallow, maybe six inches deep, but cold. How long before he got so cold he couldn't hang on any longer?

Mike, still holding the heather clump, stuck his other arm into the peat banking below it. Could he get some leverage from it? No, no, and no again. His arm held for a moment, then slid through it like through soft, wet mud.

Okay, focus. Hold the heather, keep calm and take a deep breath. Boxer then stuck her nose over the ledge, looking down at him. Mike beckoned her closer. Crouching down, she braced herself. He grabbed her front left leg with his hand, and she squealed. He saw her bloodied leg; the bullet had gone through the loose skin near her shoulder. He released it and held her other leg. She seemed to bear the pain.

Mike stroked her head, telling her, 'You beautiful Boxer.' They took a long look at each other, a mutual recognition of what a shit show they were in the middle of. The only thing keeping Mike alive at that moment was his Boxer. He could kiss her, but all he could actually do at that moment was hold on to her and hope the heather root didn't break.

Right, he thought, keep holding Boxer and try again to reach up as far as possible to grab what's left of the heather and pull slowly and evenly. He started to lift out of the bog, but the heather broke again.

Both were now slipping towards death, but they stopped inches away from Boxer joining Mike in the quagmire. Slow-motion drowning! Might have been better to have got shot, thought Mike. It was only a matter of time before he had to let Boxer go. That way only one of them was going to die today.

Mike's jacket was all but off, so he tried spreading it so he had something to press down on. It worked a bit; he pushed down on it and managed to grasp the heather root again.

Mike looked into Boxer's eyes. She was trying her best to stay strong.

In the distance, Mike saw something moving. Had they decided to come back and shoot him? Caught in silhouette against the horizon was the young Doberman, and it was closing on them. He could see it was a hundred yards away now and seemed to be running in loops. As it approached, Mike could see it had lost its collar and was bloodied. It seemed lost, scared and unsure.

Mike wondered whether it was going to come and attack them, but there was no sign of aggression. He decided to try one last, desperate ploy. He started making an overt fuss of Boxer, stroking and praising her. Feeding her a little of a wet squashed bacon butty that he retrieved from his pocket. He did this for minutes, banking on the Doberman, although fierce on the outside, having been loved by somebody enough to want to seek it again.

It was now yards away. Mike could see it from the corner of his eye but didn't want to spook it, so he didn't look at it directly. He kept making a fuss of Boxer. The Doberman sniffed around them, but Mike kept ignoring it. Boxer did the same. Thank god, thought Mike. Was it her sixth sense kicking in?

The young Doberman was now beside them. Mike kept stroking, praising and feeding Boxer, then one in three strokes went to the Doberman. Would he get bitten? Would Boxer's jealous side erupt? No. Mike kept stroking the two dogs, feeding the last morsel to the Doberman. He thought, it's now or never! He needed to grab both dogs firmly. If he missed, the Doberman would most likely run for the hills, never to come back. Mike was cold, wet and getting stiffer all the time. Would it bite? Where to grab it – the front leg, the back of its neck?

Mike decided to grab the loose skin at the back of the Doberman's neck. He got it. The shock made both dogs pull back, and he went with them. They pulled again, and Mike was free from the quagmire. Mike kissed them both, and the dogs ran and bounced around each other like friends.

'Whoa, whoa, and whoa again!' He hugged them both. 'My beauties.'

As Mike clambered up the side of the gully, he saw the thing he'd tripped on as he'd jumped. He picked it up. It was a very old sign that had sunk into the peat, saying 'DANGER.' He tried to prop it up as a warning to others. Not bloody kidding, were they? he thought.

The sun was starting to go down, and they needed to move. He could just see the Land Rover, which was still in the ditch. There appeared to be nobody around, but he couldn't be sure. Mike needed the stuff inside if he was to survive. He would try to go back to it.

Keeping low and moving with stealth, he approached the Land Rover, keeping a very close eye on the road in case a vehicle approached. As he got close, he could see it had been abandoned. He examined it, seeing little damage, and thought about trying to winch it out, but that would be a sure sign he was still alive.

Mike decided to get the essential stuff out: tent, bags plus the explosives locked under the floor panel. All loaded up with as much as he could carry, he moved away towards the hillside, checking again that nobody was coming and looking for a safe place to set up camp.

Boxer wasn't moving from the back of the Land Rover. Had she spotted something he'd missed? 'Yes, we can take the dog food too,' he told her.

Chapter 8

On arrival at the fishing lodge, Dave was bundled out of the grey van and thrown into a room that looked like it was used for cold storage. It had one little window at the top and a heavy steel door.

Dave sat looking around the stark white room with one small bed and a bucket in it. He thought the dog's instincts had been right; a nasty bunch of outlaws operated in this wild west. He thought it must be drugs on the missing boat, but why the rush? Why had they risked kidnapping him and Mike? It just seemed reckless.

Where was Mike? Was he still alive? Dave had heard the shots being fired. If the men needed them so badly, why were they prepared to kill Mike? Was Boxer dead as well? All these thoughts kept flying through his head along with his previous Navy training of just giving name, rank and serial number.

If he did what they wanted, they would probably kill him in the end. If he didn't do it at all, they may well kill him straightaway. Was everybody in on this, or just the head gamekeeper? He couldn't simply be a gamekeeper; this was too big. Dave looked at the big steel door. He wasn't going to get out of here. He wondered what would happen if he cried out.

Finn briefed Campbell about how the operation had gone down. 'Go back and get the other one; we may need him'.

'If he's dead?' asked Finn.

'Leave him there. Move the Land Rover before it attracts too much attention, and check it doesn't have a tracker,' Campbell responded. 'Get the sub operator; I want to speak to him,' he ordered.

Dave was dragged through and sat down in one of the outhouses. A semi-butchered sheep's carcass hung behind him on a hook, with blood still dripping into a bucket.

'Well, Mr Scott, why have you made this so difficult? We could have done this in a civilised manner, and you would have been well paid. But now you've done this and made it much more complicated.

We just need you to find our boat and the cargo that went down with it. That mini-sub you operate will find it for us, and then we can retrieve the cargo. We'll still pay you very well, and then you can go.'

'No. Mike escaped, so I'd get the fuck out of here before the police show up,' Dave replied angrily.

'Your mate isn't going anywhere. We have him.'

'Show me, and then we can talk.'

'We'll talk later, Mr Scott. You will help us; there's no doubt about that,' Campbell said in a cold, matter-of-fact way. Then, he turned and barked an order. 'Send Annie in to give the man some supper.'

Finn and Pete walked back across the moor. In the gloaming, everything was starting to look the same out there. Where was the stream? They must be able to find that? It was getting too dark, and the torches weren't helping. Pete kept getting his boots stuck in the peat bog. They would have to go back first thing in the morning.

Dave sat looking at the scuffed white wall in the room. Should he have handled things differently? Could he have avoided this? What if they'd just said yes to finding the wreck? Would they be in a better position? He didn't think so. Dave bit his bottom lip, and a tear ran down his cheek. I can't leave Poppy alone, he thought.

Dave thought of the bollocking he'd be getting from Jenny for getting himself into this mess and could see her telling him to get a grip, make a plan.

As morning came, the stream was found and traced back to the spot. A blue jacket was half in the bog, with an outstretched sleeve stuck in the peat. Pete tried to get close but immediately started sinking fast. Finn pulled him out. Nobody got out of there alive, was his overriding thought.

'Any sign of that Doberman?'

'No.'

'I knew Yana was making it too fucking soft.'

Campbell wasn't happy. 'Get a grappling hook, get the jacket out, and see if anything can be dragged up.' One jacket and a sheep's ribcage later, he was still not happy. Finn said the hook had gone down several feet, but a body could have sunk deeper. He was sure Mike must be dead. Campbell liked certainty, though, and this was not it.

Campbell's orders were to post a lookout on the hill. If they saw or suspected anything, they were to report back immediately. He sent Calum to cut the landline and mobile mast so that no message could get out. A couple of days without phone lines wasn't unusual and would get blamed on the recent storm.

Dave was dragged in again and got a similar cocktail of inducements and threats. Dave was as stubborn as they come and intelligent too. He knew they were working under a tight deadline, hence the desperation to get the cargo quickly, but didn't know why. He also knew his chances of survival were slim if he got them all they wanted straightaway.

Dave knew he had to give them something, so he opened the laptop and started going through the computer programme, using every technical term he could muster.

Finn had got Calum to look at the AUV to see if he could work it out. Calum had done one year at Aberdeen University studying electronic engineering before he'd had to return to look after his sick mother. He was also the one Campbell trusted to operate the drones they used. Calum looked at the laptop; there were ten screens, when he was used to only one, and the only adjustment he knew of to operate the sonar was changing the clicks. This wasn't something he could pick up within the time frame they needed.

Campbell, however, was a man who knew how to get results, even in the most difficult of circumstances. Looking through Dave's wallet and phone showed him the way ahead.

Chapter 9

The Birdfield boarding school in Wiltshire was costing Dave a small fortune; most of money he earnt went into paying the fees and the seemingly vast amounts of extra stuff that accompanied each termly bill. The Navy had picked up the cost when he was deployed to the Far East, but now he'd left it felt as if the more you paid, the shorter the terms tended to be. But Poppy loved it, and the staff had helped her so much when her mother passed. So, if she was happy, he was too.

Long gone were the days of boarding school being something to be endured. Birdfield for the most part was a haven for drawing out your full potential, whether it be academic, creative or sporting. House music and drama were ongoing evening activities, and having some parents starring in film and television made it seem that anything was possible. Poppy particularly enjoyed acting, and although she didn't have an agent like some of her friends, she thought maybe one day she might.

It was, therefore, no surprise when, at breakfast, Natalya said her uncle had a one-off role that needed to be filled urgently. It was a girl that had been kidnapped with her family. They were all going to try out for it, but Poppy fitted the role perfectly.

'Miss Black isn't going to let us go. We have to do the GCSE coursework by the weekend, and we're all behind schedule.'

'Don't worry,' Natalya said. 'We can get Ms Sharp to help. I'll speak to her in drama, period four. If we get her on side, she can persuade Miss Black to let us go.'

At lunch, Natalya was very pleased with herself. 'Ms Sharp is going to speak to Miss Black,' she said. The audition will count as part of the diploma. 'See you at 5 pm outside on the hillside.'

Five pm came, and a black transit minibus arrived. Poppy got in with Natalya and Kat. A script was given out, but improvisation was going to be encouraged. A short drive, and they arrived on the outskirts of Swindon.

As they got out, Poppy was taken into a darkened room and told to undress and put on the clothes that had been laid out for her.

She came into the studio to be greeted by Yuri, who explained what the role was: a daughter of a politician had been kidnapped so that her father would cooperate. The whole setup looked very professional.

'Lights, action, take 1.'

Two hours and many takes later. It seemed more like an interrogation than an audition. Why was she doing so many takes, and where were the other girls? Poppy was starting to get distressed; tears were running down her face.

'This is horrible. I don't like it. I want to stop.'

'Yuri said one more take. Just one – you're perfect now.'

Natalya came in to say how well she was doing, and a final take was done. Yuri was enthusiastic in his praise. 'Brilliant, fantastic, loved the tears and the red eyes.'

'That was horrible,' repeated an exhausted Poppy.

Yuri called, 'Cut. I think we have what we want.'

Natalya went crazy. 'My uncle said I was going to audition too. And Kat.'

Poppy, although a little stunned by the whole experience, watched Yuri do two very quick auditions with the other girls. 'Is that it?' asked Natalya.

'That's a wrap,' said Yuri.

In the minibus on the way back to the boarding house, Poppy listened to Natalya and Kat complain about the audition. 'We didn't even get proper makeup. Next time I see my uncle, he's going to buy me a big present for this.'

The clip was edited and uploaded.

Dave was now ready to do whatever Campbell wanted, but he was going to do it slowly to play for time.

Chapter - 10

Mike had pitched the tent when it was getting dark, placing it well back from the road and about two miles from where they had been ambushed. The fishing lodge, he thought, was about four miles away.

As dawn broke, Mike surveyed the landscape and chose a better spot, a dip between two small rises which gave him suitable cover. It was also very close to a hilltop, giving him an excellent view of the road and anybody approaching.

A camo ghillie net was put over the tent, and a few bits of heather and moss were added to make it pretty much invisible unless you were right on top of it.

The night had been cool, and the chill had taken a while to leave Mike's body. Both dogs had slept well but needed patching up. Boxer had a flesh wound, which was easy to clean and patch up. The Doberman had bite marks on her neck, which seemed to be healing, and possibly a couple of cracked ribs from where she'd been kicked, plus a nasty head wound that needed cleaning out. After a bit of moaning and dodging, they were fixed up with iodine and sticking plaster. The Doberman may need stitches at some point, Mike thought, but the superglue he'd used seemed to be holding. Both dogs seemed happy to lie down and recuperate.

Mike felt completely out of his depth. Never in his wildest dreams had he thought he'd be shot at, and the prospect of taking on an armed militia to get Dave back was frankly bonkers. Mike's recent experiences of confrontation were at a school parents' meeting when angry parents took it as a personal insult when their offspring had broken school rules and were being held accountable, or arguing with his ex-girlfriend that setting up a bomb-disposal venture with his pal was nearly as stupid as him previously wanting to enter the Isle of Man TT race.

He needed a simple, achievable plan, which was to get to a phone and call Toby for some backup. The men had taken his mobile phone when he and Dave were ambushed, so a landline would need to be accessed.

Slowly moving to the top of the hill, Mike took out the binoculars he had retrieved from the Land Rover. He could see the road clearly below, and parts of the fishing lodge. He looked hard at the likely spots for watchmen, in case they were now searching for him, and caught sight of something that he initially thought could be a piece of driftwood at the end of the headland. Mike kept looking at it, wondering if his eyes were playing tricks, but when that person was relieved by another, it was clear it was a well-concealed dugout. Mike wondered why they thought he was still alive. He continued to scan the tops of two other hilltops that had the best fields of vision, and that showed another person on top of the highest one, hiding behind a cairn. He had revealed himself wafting away midges, which had emerged from the heather as the wind had died down.

As Mike continued to scan the lookouts, it occurred to him that if he was still teaching, he would have a double period of Y11 science. He had really enjoyed teaching, even the challenge of teenagers on a Friday afternoon when they were desperate for the freedom of the weekend motivated him to achieve great exam results for all his pupils. But all that had changed one day when a pupil from another class came into his sixth-form lesson. The boy was being pursued by a physical education teacher who thought he had marked his new car with a knife, and Mike feared the teacher was going to take the boy away and hurt him. Mike wouldn't let the PE teacher take the boy because of the furious state he was in, and told him to go away. The PE teacher returned with the head of year, who Mike tried to get a commitment of the boy's safety from, but Mike just didn't believe his vague reassurances. Mike refused to hand over the boy and instead called the boy's parents to pick him up.

Mike had got his letter of suspension the next day. It was only weeks later, after the pupils had lobbied the head teacher and the press had got hold of the story, that they offered Mike his job back, but Mike had already made plans with Dave for their new venture.

Mike thought that if he was to try to rescue Dave, it might be possible to get past the first position on the headland by going along the shoreline when the tide was out. The position was still very exposed, but night-time would make it easier. Mike wasn't sure he had the nerve for that, though, so that route would be a last resort. And the hilltop lookout would be even harder to evade if the watcher was at all vigilant.

Mike's plan B, he decided, was to be so obvious you're not obvious. Dave had once told him about one of his comrades who had donned some ethnic robes and walked into a nearby enemy village, disabled the communication network and casually walked out again, with nobody noticing. He therefore knew it was possible.

He thought he could try posing as a lost walker or a tourist that thought the fishing lodge must be a hotel. That must happen to them occasionally, even out here. He didn't like the odds, though, and it would give him little room for escape if rumbled. He needed another option.

Go route one, he thought, get to the nearest house or village. The shop by the petrol station wasn't too far away. They were obviously still looking for him, not convinced he was dead, so he had to be bold and innovative in his solution.

Dave had taken his road racing bike with him on most trips, as he was also a keen cyclist. Mike's plan was to get the bike from the Land Rover roof rack, put on full Lycra, helmet and glasses, and cycle to the local shop, about five miles away, to phone for some backup. He hoped that, even on the edge of civilization, Bradley Wiggins's and Chris Froome's fame had brought some cyclists here, wanting to cycle through the islands from the butt of Lewis on to Harris and ending up at Castlebay on the tip of Barra.

In fact, he was sure he'd seen some on the ferry coming across.

Mike made a stealthy descent to the road, recovered Dave's bike from its case on the roof of the Land Rover and hid behind a large rock while he changed his kit. The top was very tight, as he was bigger than Dave, but he managed to get it on. The shoes were even tighter, and he needed a knife-cut along the toes to get into them. He felt like a neon sign in this heather and granite landscape. Feeling very vulnerable and second-guessing his plan, he slung his leg over the bike, ready to go.

Mike knew Boxer would stay in the tent, but wasn't sure about the Doberman. If she was seen, would they just think she'd been roaming free since Finn had punished her? He had decided to camouflage the glue mark on her with a black marker pen, just in case.

Mike made a very shaky start on the bike. It was light as a feather but seemed bloody unstable until you got up a bit of speed, and even then he felt he was on a knife's edge. He also thought there must be a better way to attach shoes to pedals, as he tried clipping and unclipping them for when he had to stop. As he got going and was getting up speed, he was suddenly panicked. How on earth do you change down? He was about to do a very messy crash onto the heather when he discovered the whole brake mechanism moved to do this – crisis averted for the moment.

Mike headed towards the local store by the petrol station and was very pleased to see a couple cycling in bright Lycra coming the other way.

Mike approached the shop, and with some dread that he wouldn't be able to unclip his shoes without falling on the ground, he twisted the now-loose shoes to release the clips. One released, that would do. He slowed. Dammit, the shop was shut in the middle of the day! He stopped and looked at the sign on the door giving the times. It should be open, but it was all padlocked up. Then he noticed a sign on the fuel pumps saying, 'Power cut, not open today.' Bugger, thought Mike. He had a gut feeling it wasn't going to be easy.

Okay, keep going to the village? Maybe an islander would let him use their phone. Mike carried on, getting quite used to Dave's bike, even on this fairly undulating, narrow road. If it were anywhere else, he might even be enjoying it.

As he entered the village, he could see a woman putting out a large pile of what appeared to be blankets beside the road, which turned out to be a pile of newly woven Harris Tweed, waiting to be picked up. He stopped to ask if there was a phone he could use. After being greeted in Gaelic and uttering many apologies about not having any Gaelic and how he should really learn some, he was told the lines had just gone down, probably due to the recent storm, and would probably take a few days to be back up. He asked if she had a mobile phone?

'No, my a *luaidh* (darling), the signal is so bad hardly anybody bothers. You'll have to cross back to the main island to get any chance of a signal.'

Tapadh leat was thank you. Mike now had two words of Gaelic.

The bike-riding was going well, despite the abundance of sheep droppings and the occasional car that seemed to have no desire to stop or even bother with number plates.

Getting to the crossing was proving remarkably easy, as Mike got familiar with the bike. The hills weren't too steep, and he was getting used to the gearing, which made all the difference. As the causeway approached, a single figure could be seen. Mike stopped to get a map out and pretended to be looking at it while he wondered whether he should try his luck and cross the causeway. He then saw one of the cars he'd seen at the fishing lodge, half concealed behind some rocks. Was that a stick or a rifle the man was holding?

Beside the causeway were now some road signs saying, 'Repairs to crossing, no access to the island.' A sudden ferocious incoming shower saw the figure race to the car for shelter. It was a rifle he'd been holding. This gave Mike the distraction he needed to head back to the tent, thoroughly soaked to the skin.

Being greeted by two dogs was a little bit of a surprise, but a completely destroyed rucksack was not, with both dogs looking into the air. Nothing to do with them boss, no idea how that happened.

Chapter 11

Mike broke the seal on a ration pack and waited for it to heat up. He felt his options were limited; he could hope the phone lines being down was nothing to do with Campbell and cycle back to the shop. But in his gut, he felt that was wishful thinking. He could try to swim the gap between the two islands, but getting down the cliff face in one piece would be a miracle, and even if he made it down, there appeared to be some fierce tidal currents. He just didn't know if he was a strong enough swimmer to make it across without his usual diving gear, which had been taken with their boat.

As he dipped his fork into the now-hot stew, with the undivided attention of both dogs, he decided he would scout out the fishing lodge and see if it would be possible to get Dave out. Mike would need to take the dogs with him, or there may not be a tent left to come back to.

Once fed, they set off, all three camouflaged in makeshift ghillie suits, looking a little funny, but it was essential to blend in with their surroundings as it was still light. Boxer was not amused by this indignity, but she was going to put up with it this one time. The Doberman needed to be kept an eye on, as she was drawn to each sheep they passed.

Moving to the headland opposite the fishing lodge, he used small hillocks to cover his advance. As he came around the tip of the headland, Mike found a great vantage point and was pretty certain he hadn't been spotted by either of the lookouts. Through his binoculars, he could see they were now drinking from a flask and eating snacks. They were clearly getting bored and being far less careful about concealing themselves. They must think he was dead; that should give him a bit of breathing space, at least.

Mike scanned the fishing lodge. He could see very little happening. A few figures were preparing vegetables in the kitchen. There was no sign of the RIB or Dave.

At 5.30, two minibuses arrived in front of the lodge. The binoculars were proving excellent at picking out every detail. The fishers had arrived back from their beats with their day's catch; it was being laid out on a table by the ghillies, and Campbell was weighing each fish and recording it.

As Mike made fine adjustments to the binoculars, it suddenly started to look like the Oscars of fishing. He couldn't make them all out, but there was the ex-foreign minister who had just resigned with the king of one of the Gulf States, the Irish football coach and Peter Dawson, the anti-religion author.

Mike wondered if Dawson knew about the cinema and the commotion caused by the religious fundamentalists. Probably not. He thought if the author had joined them at the cinema, there might have been spontaneous combustion.

The tax-dodging Jones brothers, who owned the Courier newspaper, looked like they'd had a good day and were already on the champagne. This seemed to be fishing royalty, with the recently notorious Prince John topping the list, although he didn't seem to have caught as many fish as the others.

Campbell had greeted them all, the champagne was flowing, triple whiskies were downed, and it appeared to have been an excellent day's sport. Photos were being taken as they stood beside their catches.

As things moved inside, all appeared to be normal. The kitchen was in full flow, with dinner being served by girls in short waitress outfits. They appeared to be having five or six courses with a different type of alcoholic drink accompanying each one, and most had a large brandy in hand as they left the dining room. Evening discussions had started, and card games were being played and newspapers read, ironed conveniently into tabloid size.

Campbell met with Prince John in his office, where he appeared to be giving the prince a gift of a fishing rod, which he had pieced together and seemed to be pressing on the ceiling for some reason. The prince was thanking him profusely.

Then Mike heard the familiar sound of an outboard. Was that their outboard? It was currently a way off but was heading slowly towards the lodge. As it emerged from around the headland, Mike could make out Dave and two others. They docked the boat and climbed ashore at the jetty. There was a clear silhouette of a gun pointing in Dave's direction. They were heading towards the back of the lodge to a meeting room, which was visible through the now-lit windows. Gestures were made, indicating nothing had yet been found. The men disappeared for a few minutes and then returned without Dave, suggesting he was being held in a room at the back of the lodge.

Getting much closer to the lodge was going to be the only way if an escape plan was at all realistic.

Mike knew he would need to keep watching, but he sat back for a quick snack that he shared with the dogs. As the night progressed, with the lights on in the lodge and the curtains open, most of the comings and goings could be clearly observed through the binoculars.

Both dogs had been sound asleep for a while, resting against each other and Mike in the small dip that was concealing them. They occasionally woke and often snored. Mike was also getting rather tired and starting to drift off. Suddenly, there were eight eyes looking directly at him, surrounding them. Mike nearly had a heart attack. How had he not heard them approach? Holy shit, no way out of this. Then came an equally sudden realisation that nothing had happened. It was four sheep. Thank Christ. Boxer looked up with some disdain. Of course they're sheep, and she also seemed to have a vague hope that she could have some fun chasing them away. The moment the sheep realised there were two dogs, they were gone with the wind.

Having observed that all was quiet at the lodge – the last lights had gone out at about 1 am in the guest lounge, after what appeared to be a high-stakes game of backgammon — Mike took the dogs back to the tent and prepared to do some close scouting.

Mike kept asking himself, was it sensible? Was it too dangerous? Was there an easier alternative? What if he set an alarm off? There was no way he could take on one of those ex-military guys, never mind two. This thought was rapidly followed by others: it's only a scouting trip, it's the middle of the night, and they think you're dead. Dave would do the same for you. Just one step at a time.

The wind had risen a little, so it was going to be a challenging but doable swim. Mike wished he had his wetsuit, but that had been taken with the RIB, so it would be boxer shorts and a black bin liner with dry clothes in it dragged behind.

Swimming in the middle of the night was never a good idea, and as he got into the cold water, he started being dragged away from his route across by a tidal current. Thank goodness it was the middle of summer, as even at this late hour, there was still some light to see by. The compass on his watch was also a big help.

As he swam through the seaweed on the far shore, he was feeling a little exhausted and had swallowed a bit too much seawater. When he made land, he dried off as best he could and put on some navy-blue base layers, which rendered him almost invisible, smearing some peat on his face for final effect.

Coming over the back wall and through the woods seemed the best bet. Would there be any tripwires? Or was it too big an area, with sheep and rabbits around to set them off too often, for them to bother? The ex-military launch was certainly silently rigged to alert them to intruders. Mike and Dave had spotted that when they'd first arrived to deal with the mine. That now seemed an age ago.

The substantial wall surrounding the lodge was made of dry stone and appeared to be crumbling in places. Mike wanted to avoid knocking any rocks out and causing any noise. Picking what looked like the strongest, most even part, he climbed up and over. As he landed, a huge, dark figure immediately rose up before him. Fight or flight kicked in instantly as he raced through the wood, looking for cover. As he turned back, he saw the silhouette of a golden eagle rise in the sky. It had been eating the carcass of a dead sheep.

Mike looked around, sighed with relief and took a long, slow breath. Had he yelped with fear? If so, somebody could be coming out of the lodge soon. He couldn't remember doing it, but that eagle had scared the shit out of him. It was like the huge black wings of death coming straight for him. Heart calmed, well hidden, and with nobody emerging from the lodge, it seemed he had got away with it.

Crawling along the walled garden at the back of the lodge, he could make out four small windows high up on the ground floor, too small to crawl through and with bars across them. There was also a small, metal, spiral staircase to a fire door on the first floor, with many white dots on the ground below that must be cigarette butts. Getting any closer was going to be tough without the outside lights coming on automatically.

Although it was very early, dawn was starting to break through, as this far north in the summer the nights were very short.

Chancing his arm in the half-light, thinking that the movement sensor activating the automatic light wouldn't make much difference, he pulled himself up to the windowsill and looked through the first barred window. He could see the end of a bed and someone's feet, then the same in the next room. The third was a toilet and the fourth empty. He thought it too risky to knock or call through the window without knowing who was in which room. Had they got two prisoners?

Although only 4 am, it was starting to get very light. Moving quickly back towards the shore, Mike checked out the surrounding outbuildings: the small hatchery, the garage and the boathouse.

Mike thought Dave could only be in the lodge, in one of those two barred, windowed rooms. But with about forty people in the fishing lodge between guests and staff, it was going to be near impossible to enter without being caught.

Mike swam back across to the headland, this time in almost glass-like sea conditions. The sea was so smooth he worried that he might be quite visible if somebody was up that early and looking in his direction.

Getting out of the water and into the heather, there were clouds of midges everywhere, biting every exposed area of his flesh. The wildlife on this island was starting to do his head in.

Moving with stealth back to the tent, it was clear to him that this was not going to be an easy extraction. Was it even possible?

Chapter 12

As Campbell looked at the laptop data that Calum was showing him, with all its space-age three-dimensional graphics, and heard the debrief from Pete, it was clear to him that Dave was doing what they wanted.

A huge area had been covered during the fifteen hours of searching on the first day. It was also clear how tight a deadline they were working to and that it was closing fast. Dave assumed that must be to do with the week-long stays that most of the fishermen had booked. 'Two more days. You must get it in two more days,' Dave could just hear Campbell saying to Pete.

Dave had made it clear he would only continue if he knew Poppy was safe. Campbell had anticipated this, so another quick video was played. Dave was relieved but had a sense that something wasn't right. Was it his imagination playing tricks or the trauma of the last couple of days? He couldn't decide, but something kept niggling at the back of his mind.

Finn had been debriefed by his two lookouts that nobody had been seen. One he trusted completely, the other not so much. Something about some cyclists was hazy, but they were becoming a more common sight, especially in the summer.

'Rory, give it another day to see if anything turns up. Alastair, I need you to get the Land Rover out of the ditch before anybody starts asking questions. Don't take it back to the lodge; just park it in that small stone quarry near where he went in the bog for the police to find,' said Finn.

'What about the Doberman? The locals may kick off if it starts killing their sheep,' said Rory.

'It'll come back when it's hungry,' was Finns reply.

The atmosphere at the fishing lodge was more business-like and less tense than the last couple of days. Campbell seemed reassured by the data he'd seen. The boat must be very close to being found. Some of the ghillies were also back playing pool, despite the carpet retaining the remnants of

Kristijonas's blood — an ominous reminder of who they were working for.

The day for Dave started again at 5 am. The sea was calm; the sky was clear. The sea loch looked just beautiful at this time of day. The GPS located the point where they had stopped the day before, and they continued the search. An hour passed and then two. The sky darkened a little, and the wind picked up, but not to a level to concern them, just a bit of gloom to go with Dave's mood.

What would happen if and when he found the wreck? They didn't seem to care too much about the man they'd lost, so he didn't rate his chances. Was Poppy going to be alright? Would he have a chance to escape when he went diving to bring up the lost cargo? Were they expecting him to do it on his own, or would some of their crew also dive? All these thoughts were going through his mind when the screen changed. The sunken boat had been found, and it looked like a body was attached to it.

Pete radioed back to the lodge, as they hadn't discussed what they would do when they found the wreck. A broken signal wasn't helping make sense of the conversation. 'Just get the cargo up,' was the gist of the message. The body could wait.

Pete asked Dave, 'How do we get the cargo up?' and a quick discussion was had. It would take several trips; as the weight was too much for the RIB, the launch from the lodge was going to be needed. Dave was to do it all himself, which surprised him a little.

He donned his diving gear and started the dive. It would be so easy to escape now, he thought, but how to make Poppy safe? He was sure the moment he got everything up, he would be dead. He imagined being hit over the head as the last package was recovered, left to die – just another unfortunate diving accident.

Dave decided he needed to hide some of the cargo so they would need him for another day. But which bit to hide, and where? The small bales wrapped in white plastic were obviously cocaine or something similar, but he doubted the men would have kidnapped them and killed Mike just for that.

He thought those bales would have been too much of a risk, so the items wrapped in black plastic were the ones to go for. Six packages. He thought he could hide two of them with the aid of a suitable distraction. Choosing which two was going to be pot luck. If they were watching the laptop screen, they would see Dave doing it, so he needed something that would divert their attention elsewhere.

The body floating up from the bow of the boat could be the distraction he needed. Angus had caught his foot between a metal fuel pipe and the gunwale and hadn't been able to free himself in time. It looked like he'd tried to cut his shoe off and cut into his foot doing it.

As Dave looked closely at Angus's body, he knew he had a suitable distraction.

He got the crowbar he'd used to open the hold and levered the fuel pipe. The body shot up to the surface. It was covered with little inch-wide orange crabs, and as the body hit the surface, they stayed for a moment, then scurried off, revealing a face eaten down to the bone. The eyes were staring out; the hair was moving, and then the scalp fell off as the crabs underneath left the skull.

Suitably shocked, distracted and intrigued, the men put out a boathook to catch the body. As they did that, some of the clothes slipped off, along with about two hundred little crabs.

The launch from the lodge slowly pulled the body away to the nearby shore, as trying to lift it out might see it all fall apart and leave less space for the recovered cargo.

By the time all this was done, Dave had hidden two of the smaller black bags and had come up to the surface with another one to be taken on board.

The recovery of the cargo continued well into the afternoon. The white bales were offloaded onto two small fishing boats, which then left. There were two large, heavy packages left, and even with the advantage of being underwater, they were proving too heavy for Dave and had to be slowly winched up to the launch, which was tipping quite dramatically as they were dragged on board.

Dave sat wondering if he'd done enough to keep himself alive, or were the things he'd hidden of insufficient consequence? He vowed to himself that if he was still alive tomorrow and diving for the remaining cargo, he was going to make a break for it.

As they arrived back at the jetty, Dave could see Campbell speaking to Pete. Had he seen him mouth 'one more day,' or was that wishful thinking? He seemed particularly pleased with the two black bags that looked like suitcases. Had he hidden the wrong ones? Was this his last night?

Chapter 13

The idea had come to Mike in the middle of the night. It was a wild card but the only one he could see having a reasonable chance of success. Was he kidding himself? Would this work? Saying it out loud to the dogs didn't seem to reassure him or the dogs.

If it didn't work, he was going to have to try to sneak around as he had the previous night, enter the lodge, find a route to Dave's cell and expect to open or blow the lock, then get the hell out of there super-fast. Having thought about it again, he was going to have to do that anyway, just hopefully with a suitable distraction.

He needed to make some kind of poster, and all that was at hand was an A4 pad of yellow paper Dave had been making notes on with his black marker. It would have to do. He made five posters and rolled them up carefully.

Mike got Dave's bike out again and donned the cycling kit, struggling even more to get into the still-damp Lycra top.

He headed for the village with his makeshift posters.

Were the dogs going to behave themselves, get so bored they would shred everything or go wandering? Little was going to stop them doing that if they decided to.

The posters looked as good as you could hope for, considering they were done by hand with a thick black marker. They read, 'Talk by Peter Dawson tonight, 8 pm, at Gumerston Fishing Lodge. WHY GOD DOES NOT EXIST. All welcome.' Judging by the recent cinema experience, this could do the trick. Even a couple of cars turning up might be enough of a distraction; a dozen would be perfect. Would they contact others on the main island to come along or just throw the posters in the bin with a few curses chasing after them?

Mike posted one on the noticeboard by the shop, another in the middle of the village, and the final one was pinned to the front door of the church!

On the way back to the tent, it was clear the men had given up on him being alive. Mike had spotted one lookout that morning, but on the way back, nobody at all. This should make things a little easier, he thought.

He was also surprised to spot the Land Rover in a little quarry, something to be checked out later if there was time, not a trap to walk into now.

As Mike got back to the tent, both dogs seemed well recovered and eager to play, and Mike felt relaxed enough to spend half an hour playing 'pull the rest of the rucksack to bits' with them behind the cover of the hill.

Mike knew this was it, tonight or never. His mind kept spinning with all the possibilities. He knew he should be hungry, but he wasn't. He took a sip of water and checked everything again: explosive charges, one knife he hoped not to have to use and his watch for navigation, which had charged a little from the solar cells, but not a lot. He taped a crowbar to his leg. Had he forgotten anything?

As he left the dogs for the second time that day, he wondered if he would ever see them again. He was getting quite fond of the Doberman, and Boxer could tell. He briefly thought that maybe leaving teaching hadn't been the wisest choice; but if he survived, what a story!

The water was just as cold tonight, but, due to the breeze, there were no midges. He smeared bike grease on his face and started swimming. His route was going to be longer tonight, as it was still light and he needed to be further away from the fishing lodge. Would his time calculations be right with this extra distance?

Mike crawled out of the water after a long swim and got under the sea bank as quickly as possible to catch his breath. He felt much more exposed in the daylight. Making his way slowly towards the lodge, his head was constantly moving back and forth for any sign of Campbell's men or other dogs. This was bloody risky, he thought; maybe going in the dead of night would have been the better option. At least the RIB was tied up, so Dave must be in the lodge.

Suddenly, there were cars arriving: one, then two, four in total, heading for the front of the lodge, lights flashing, horns beeping. The islanders must have taken some Dutch courage to face the godless one. Game on, game sodding on, thought Mike, as he now rushed to get into position. A party of about a dozen islanders got out of the cars, marched through the front door of the lodge and shouted, 'Where is the godless one? Where is he?'

Dawson was sitting in the lounge with a glass of whiskey, discussing fishing tactics for the next day. It embarrassed him that this was happening with the other fishing guests around and about, and he tried to usher the islanders outside. For a moment, it went quite still; it was as if the villagers had finally seen pure evil and didn't know what to do. Some were making cross signs and muttering to themselves; others were spitting on the carpet. The church elder who had come with them was chanting some prayer at Peter Dawson.

Colonel Bentley stood up. 'I don't know what's going on chaps, but you need to leave. This is private property. I'll call the police if you don't.'

One of the waitresses had shot off to get help.

A sudden rush of bodies arrived in the foyer, where Peter Dawson had gone to try and talk them round, which seemed less likely than a lottery win.

Finn arrived in a hurry. Looking at the group, he walked over and head butted the biggest of the bunch, who went down like a stone. The group was now backing away, carrying their fallen friend and cursing Finn. A woman dressed in black called Finn 'Godless scum' and spat at him. She was unconscious by the time the spittle had landed. Curses were being hurled as they got into their cars in retreat. One man, who had a handful of stones ready to hurl, thought better of it and resorted to a call of 'God will judge you all' as he closed his door.

This was all happening too early. Mike had put 8 pm on the poster, and it was barely 7.30. He was going to have to move fast, take some risks and hope.

Mike dashed around the back of the lodge to the spiral staircase where the first-floor fire door was open. Shit, somebody was standing there, smoking. Then a whole cigarette was flung to the ground, and they were gone.

Mike scurried up the external staircase and entered the building through the fire door. Quickly looking left and right to see if it was clear, he cautiously stepped down the stairs. He could now see the two doors he wanted, but both were shut. He felt for the explosive devices in his bag. Which lock to blow, or should he do them both? Then he suddenly saw the keys, large as life, hanging from a hook by each door.

Mike turned the key to the first door, hoping it was Dave in there.

'God, I thought you were dead,' Dave said. Mike gestured to keep quiet and to come with him.

Dave pointed at his feet – no shoes – and then pointed to the room next door. As they started to move, a clear voice was heard. 'Take me too, or I scream.' Slightly frozen, Dave just took the key and opened the door to reveal a raven-haired young woman. She was dressed in jogging bottoms and a T-shirt. Dave pointed to both their bare feet. She slipped next door and back in seconds with some of the ghillies' boots and jackets. She gestured, pointing several times to the end of the corridor, where Mike saw another fire door behind some old chairs. It was stiff but opened, and they rushed past the outbuildings, catching a glimpse of the ruckus still going on in front of the lodge.

Mike told Dave and the woman to go along the seashore and to stick close to the bank, which was shaded. The fading light was helping to cover their escape. Dave gestured to Mike, what are you doing? Mike pointed at the boat. Dave whispered, 'Risky.'

'It's all bloody risky,' Mike whispered back.

Moving along the bank, the woman said 'Down, down!' quietly but urgently. Dave looked around. He couldn't see anything, even though the girl was pointing, and when Dave went to move forward, she yanked his collar, and he fell flat on his back. He was mad as hell and about to lose his cool, when he suddenly caught sight of the neck-high wire he was just about to walk into.

Mike slipped into the water, headed for the RIB and untied it. He swam a few strokes as he pulled it towards the shore. Up to his neck in water, Mike slowly walked the boat away from the lodge and along the shore, carefully looking back to see if anybody had noticed a boat slowly moving away. No. Now out of sight of the lodge, he dragged the boat as quickly as possible to where Dave and the woman were standing, barely visible under the banking.

Mike showed Dave the charges he'd brought with him to blast the door locks and pointed at the large launch that was anchored in front of the lodge.

'It's alarmed,' Dave said.

Mike nodded. 'Be careful. Five, ten minutes. How long for the timer? Ten, okay?'

Dave put his thumb up.

Mike changed the digital setting and set off swimming as quietly as possible. A head popped up; a big brown grey seal's eyes looked back at Mike. They regarded each other for a moment. Mike was now starting to get used to wildlife appearing at crucial moments, like they were checking up on his progress.

The launch's alarm lines were difficult to see. If you didn't know they were there, you'd never notice them. Mike dipped under one line, moving slowly forward, and placed one charge on the side of the launch. It didn't seem to be as secure as he wanted, and he worried about it getting swept off with the force of the water, so he opted to move it and placed it on the underside of the large outboard motor. He put the second charge on the motor shaft and then moved off slowly and quietly.

Mike could just about hear Campbell talking with Colonel Bentley. 'What set this off? How did they know Dawson was here? This can't happen again. The gate needs to be locked so it's not possible for it to be lifted off its hinges.'

Campbell nodded. Was this a coincidence? He didn't like coincidences. Campbell left Colonel Bentley and apologised to Mr Dawson, saying he hoped it wouldn't spoil the rest of his trip.

'Maybe a chapter for my next book,' Dawson replied with a wry smile.

Campbell walked towards Finn, then looked down at what appeared to be someone's dropped litter. He picked up the scrunched piece of paper, unfolded it, and read the poster.

Mike was a quarter of the way back to the RIB when he heard 'bugger' ring out, then 'bugger' again when Campbell saw the RIB had gone.

How the men got to the launch so quickly, Mike didn't know, but a ten-minute timer now seemed to be far too long. This was going to be a chase, and they had the faster boat. How quickly were they going to be able to catch up on a half-mile advantage?

Mike knew he wouldn't get back to the RIB in time and signalled to Dave. Dave and Mike both knew they had to go now. Mike was fairly sure they hadn't seen him, so there was a chance he could get back to the far shore and the dogs.

Both boats set off flat-out, hitting the fairly large waves like hammer blows. Dave moved the boat as close to the shore as possible, giving them a little extra speed in the calmer water but also raising the chances of hitting any rocks just below the surface. The woman watched as bullets flew off the water to the side of the boat.

Whack! As the boat's hull hit a rock just under the water, Dave lifted the outboard just in time for it to miss the rocks, or the propeller would have been wrecked. Flying off the reef, the boat hit the water hard and lost control for a moment. The launch was closing on them.

More bullets. This time, they hit the RIB, puncturing a couple of sections on the side of the boat. Dave was still pushing as hard as he dared. Water was starting to come over the side of the boat where it was punctured, and the bottom was starting to fill with water. Dave shouted to the woman, 'Pull the plug! Pull the plug at the bottom of the boat!' The woman looked back, puzzled. Surely that would let more water in; had she heard him right? 'Just do it,' he insisted. She did, and the water was sucked out of the bottom due to the speed of the boat moving forward.

The other boat was now closing on them fast. Had the explosive devices fallen off, or had they been found? This was proving the longest ten minutes in history. The men were now just behind them, guns raised. Was this their final breath?

The woman looked back at the launch and swore at them in Russian. A machine gun was raised towards her. *Bang.*

The explosives on the outboard motor finally blew. They knocked the shooter to the ground, and the launch ground to a halt. Dave grabbed the woman, and they lay as flat as possible as the RIB moved off, followed by a spray of bullets bouncing off the outboard motor they were hiding behind, puncturing even more of the RIB's rubber cells.

The RIB limped off, and the bullets stopped. Dave peered over the shattered casing of the outboard motor. They were now a safe distance away.

Dave turned over to look to see if the young woman was still alive. She put out her hand. 'Hi, my name is Yana.'

Dave manoeuvred what was left of the RIB around the nearby headland to get out of sight. Thank god the RIB had a buoyant fibreglass base, or they would have been at the bottom of the ocean by now.

Chapter 14

Campbell had everybody on their toes as quickly and quietly as possible. Colonel Bentley had been a very useful veneer for Campbell, giving him cover for his operation, and he wanted that to continue.

Colonel Bentley was grateful to Campbell. When he'd taken over as head of the fishing syndicate, poaching had been rife, and the annual catches had fallen sharply. Spanish trawlers and the like were taking huge catches off the coast by laying nets several miles long across the estuary, threatening to kill the salmon run completely. Campbell had turned this around, and Colonel Bentley kept getting praise for doing such a wonderful job. The catches this season in particular were amazing, so Colonel Bentley asked few questions, even when he feared Finn had overstepped the mark, like tonight.

As Dave and the woman sped away with the launch in pursuit, Mike was still in the water, hiding by one of the floats of the plane Prince John had arrived in.

Mike was cold, but he couldn't start the swim back as another boat was being taken down the jetty, ready to be launched, with several men in a good position to see him if he moved.

He knew the swim back to the shore was going to be tougher the colder he got, but with the boat being readied, he was going to have to bide his time.

As the boat took to the water in pursuit of the other two, Mike knew he had to go soon. Hoping a cloud would come over to make the diminishing light give him a bit more cover, he watched as the figures outside of the lodge slowly went back in.

Mike could see Campbell still speaking to two of the fishing guests. Then two figures appeared with packages. Were these the valuable items Dave had recovered from the wreck? They were being moved from Campbell's office. The first was a black tube being put into the boot of a Range Rover; the second, a smaller, box-shaped object, was handed over to somebody who appeared so grateful he hugged

Campbell twice. Two large suitcases were now been wheeled from the office into a rowing boat that was heading straight for the plane Mike was under. Time to go.

Swimming as smoothly as he could, Mike started the swim back. He'd done it three times now, so he knew where the currents were. He wondered what was in the two suitcases heading for Prince John's plane. Was it money? That seemed unlikely for somebody so rich, but, if you believed the tabloids, it wouldn't be the first time he'd accepted suitcases full of cash. If it was drugs, surely nobody needed two suitcases worth. Prince John had more jewels and antiques than half of the UK. What the hell was it? Whatever it was, it seemed bloody heavy.

Nobody seemed to be looking for him, which was great. He was making good progress back to the shore. His swimming had certainly improved, and he wondered why he didn't do it more at home. As he progressed, his arms ached and his legs were cramping occasionally, so he switched between swimming strokes. As he swam, he kept wondering whether Dave had made it. Had the explosive devices gone off? Who was the woman, and why was she locked up? He could now see his landing spot on the shore, and that dark cloud he had prayed for was now overhead, which would give him cover as he got out.

It was only then that he started to realise he was losing all feeling in his body. He could see his arms moving in front of him but couldn't feel any connection to them. Mike looked at his feet to see if they were still moving. Thankfully, they were, but only just. The cold was starting to seize his whole body up.

Slight panic was setting in. Was he going to just stop and sink to the bottom? He thought as long as he could see his arms moving he would be okay, slow but okay. Hitting the last of the currents where he usually had to strengthen his stroke to get through, he was going nowhere, like an LP stuck on the same groove. Shit, was this it?

He could just see what he thought was a buoy. At least he'd be able to hold on to it, to gather any last strength to push through. Not a buoy, must be that seal again. Oh my god, it's Boxer! Putting his arm around her, he kicked as hard as he could for the shore, hoping there was some movement left in his body, using his other arm to plough through the water. It was like trying to get a drunk person up some stairs: slow, hard, almost impossible. Mike finally hit the shore. As he crawled out, he just wanted to lie down and stop, to collapse. He knew if he did that, though, he would likely die from hypothermia.

Still not feeling his body, he clambered ashore, tripping over a couple of times until he got used to watching his legs move one at a time in front of him. He was walking like some zombie.

Mike knew he must get back to the tent, get dry and get some warmth. He struggled back towards the tent on the hillside, which wasn't a steep slope, but it felt like he was climbing a mountain. Holding Boxer's collar kept him moving forward. He stopped several times on the way up, as his body kept suggesting he just stop and sleep. It was seducing him with thoughts that it would be so pleasant and comforting to rest a while. Thankfully, there was a still louder voice in his head telling him to keep going or die, but it was getting quieter.

As Mike finally got to the tent, he just had the strength to get out of his wet clothes and collapse under some dry ones, with the dogs on either side. He still had no feeling in his body, but he hugged them close for warmth. If somebody came now, that would be it. He couldn't move. Almost an hour later, the feeling in Mike's body started to come back. God, that had been close.

Chapter 15

Dave was nursing the RIB around the headland as the waves started to overwhelm them. Shelter from the estuary had given way to the open sea. The foam buoyancy cells in the fibreglass hull were all that were keeping them afloat, and the outboard engine, although sounding pretty ropy, was by some miracle still running. They were going to run out of fuel fast, though, even at this slow pace.

While they were looking desperately for a spot to land where they could get out safely, a line of rocks leading up to the outside of a village appeared. The RIB was now very difficult to manoeuvre, and the stronger winds weren't helping. Dave thought just getting the RIB above those rocks would give them some shelter, and the wind would then push them ashore. Just about then, the outboard started to splutter. It was sucking up the last dregs of fuel. It then stopped. They were drifting.

As the RIB drifted towards the line of rocks, they would have to jump out onto them, because if they missed their chance, Dave feared the RIB would keep drifting into the middle of the sea.

'Jump! We have to jump, girl!'

Jumping, Yana landed like a gymnast, Dave less so, smacking his knee and arm against the rocks.

The RIB drifted off, then snagged on a rock, with the wind buffeting it about as the waves crashed over it.

They gathered their breath and looked at each other; both were soaked to the skin. Dave's arm was dripping with blood.

'Rocks, not bullets,' Dave replied to her look. 'We need to get out of here and maybe get a car from the village.'

They looked around, seeing a small harbour filled with a variety of fishing boats. Yana pointed to a track that was carved like a corridor dug deep into the steep hillside.

'Let's follow that?'

Dave nodded. Climbing up, they could see two buildings and a truck parked between them, and then three figures appeared. Shit, did they just survive all that to get caught again?

Dave had decided he was going to go down fighting. He would rather die here than get captured again and then disposed of when Campbell was done with him.

Then a woman's voice, 'Come quickly, come quickly before they get here!' Someone was helping them. Why were they helping them?

The pair were ushered to a house and on up some stairs, into a kitchen. Donald introduced himself, his wife Cathy and their son Donald-John, before the two men left the kitchen.

'Why are you helping us?' Dave asked Cathy.

'My husband saw them trying to kill you. Anybody that's an enemy of theirs is a friend of ours. Evil men, evil men. You must get changed, or you'll catch your death. I'll get you some clothes.'

Dave asked where her husband and son had gone. 'They've gone to get what's left of your boat and hide it.'

'Is there a phone?' Dave asked. 'I must get hold of my daughter to see if she's safe.'

'The phones are out; they say it was the storm, but they went down a day later! You'll need to get to the main island.'

Yana looked at Dave and said, 'Your daughter is safe.'

'How do you know? How do you know that?'

Yana explained what had happened and that Finn was so impressed by Campbell's plan and execution that he'd boasted to her about it.

'I knew there was something not right about it. It niggled me. I couldn't make it out, but yes, it looked too professional.'

Dave asked again, 'Are you sure? He wasn't just messing with you? If he can do that, they can still get to her. I must get back.'

Cathy explained that although the locals never liked the outsiders from the fishing estate, the villagers had reluctantly worked for them, as there were hardly any other jobs on the island. The arrangement had worked fine for many years until Campbell arrived, and then it all changed for the worse.

'They make our children do evil things for them, and if they don't, they disappear.'

Dave asked, 'Don't the police help?'

'The police won't take them on. They're in their pocket or too scared – probably both – so they just report "lost at sea" when somebody goes missing,' said Cathy.

'I thought you only spoke Gaelic,' Dave stated.

'No, we all speak English, just not to them,' Cathy replied.

Yana and Dave went and changed, returning a little itchy from the coarse but warm wool clothing they'd been given. Cathy gave them some broth, which they downed along with some soused herring and thick homemade bread.

Cathy's son and husband returned, holding the outboard motor. They had hidden the boat by covering it with rocks and peat.

Dave told them his story as they sat in silence and nodded. They'd suspected much of what he was telling them.

'There's nothing we can do, but if you get back, can you get Scotland Yard to come?'

Dave nodded but suspected it would take some convincing.

'My friend who helped us escape, we got separated. We must get to him.'

Cathy's husband Donald thought for a while, rubbed his chin and then told them an idea that might work. Although the whole of the island was owned by the fishing estate, the crofters had common grazing rights, so most of the village had sheep roaming free.

'If I go up with Bessie, my sheepdog, there's a good chance I could find him.'

'Can we all go?' asked Dave. He looked at Yana, and she nodded.

'You certainly blend in with those clothes. I'll teach you some Gaelic words in case Campbell's thugs stop us.'

Half an hour of a Gaelic lesson later, plus a strong whiskey, and it was time to sleep.

'We only have one spare bed. Are you two together?'

'No. I'll take the floor,' said Dave.

Lying on the floor, Dave asked Yana why she was locked up. Yana explained she had worked in the best nightclubs in Moscow: lots of beautiful girls, rich guys, beautiful clothes, money, presents, champagne and caviar every night – proper stuff, really expensive. Then she was asked to entertain some rich American politician she pissed off and ended up in that shithole lodge.

There was obviously a lot more to the story than that. Dave wasn't going to push his luck too much but still wanted to know.

'Why were you locked up?'

'I put Finn's whale fin on the fire. Nasty bastard stank like that whale fin too. No one hurts Yana and gets away with it.'

Chapter 16

Campbell was standing at the jetty, weighing up the situation, with too many questions unanswered. How had the outboard on the launch come off; had it not been secured properly? The motor was now at the bottom of the sea. Could it have been ripped off by hitting a rock? The engine blowing seemed very unlikely – Japanese engineering was so reliable. But how could the prisoners have sabotaged it if they were making off in the other direction with the RIB? Pete had said there were just two people in the RIB: the diver and the girl.

'Check the cells. See how they got out,' said Campbell.

Yana had escaped just a couple of days ago by persuading one of the ghillies to help her, using her considerable charms. She had then got him drunk and made it as far as the causeway, but the tide was in, and that was the day the terrible storm hit. She got apprehended waiting to cross, soaked to the skin and freezing, with the Doberman she'd befriended. Campbell thought it highly unlikely there was another member of staff who would help her after the way Pete had dealt with the ghillie. Was it the other diver who was supposed to be dead? Nobody was admitting letting her out, but Finn had been tasked with making sure that was true.

The keys were in the locks, so somebody had helped.

Campbell planned, ordered and coordinated the search from the fishing lodge. He wanted to find the boat or a body.

At dawn, he dispatched a search party of two vans to the headland, where the damaged RIB was last seen. Pete told six of the men to scour the coastline. Calum had launched a drone to get to the areas too difficult to cover on foot, but it wasn't picking up anything of interest.

They had given the launch a temporary repair and a new outboard motor and were searching the sea coast with another boat.

It looked like the boat may have sunk, so they would have had to swim for it if they were still alive.

Pete had said that the RIB had been riddled with bullets, and nobody had been visible as the boat disappeared behind the headland.

Finn was questioning the domestic staff, most of whom intensely disliked him and therefore kept their distance. That was apart from Annie, who worked in the kitchen. She had a teenage crush on Finn. He paid her little attention but enjoyed the special bits of food she would prepare for him. The other girls kept warning her about him, but all she could see was his impressive physical appearance.

When they got to the village, neither boat nor bodies had been found. The ghillies would have to go back to do their day job, helping their fishers learn the lies and catch as many salmon as they could. Most were now exhausted, having had little sleep or food.

Campbell sent one man to the lookout post on the hill, and another was sent to guard the causeway. This situation must be contained, he thought. They were so close to executing the plan.

They left three men in the village to continue to look for any evidence of the boat or its occupants.

The villagers had anticipated that Campbell's men would come, and a group of them had gathered together and were walking towards the three men, who were highlighted by the early morning sun. The crofters were going to confront them.

The men tried to enquire whether the villagers had seen a boat or any strangers, but they got short shrift. A string of Gaelic words they didn't understand was hurled at them. The message was unmistakable. They were not wanted and were certainly outnumbered.

The men really didn't want to be there in the first place and didn't want to fight their way out. With Finn or Pete at their side, they would have had no choice, but a few glances between them confirmed they were going to go back to the van and continue on to the other side of the village.

It had annoyed Campbell that two of the packages on the boat had been lost: an occult painting and an exquisite piece of jewellery from the Berlin museum heist were still on the seabed. He thought, however, that they could be retrieved at a later date, since they now knew the coordinates of the wreck; but two of the fishers would have to go home empty-handed for the moment.

He felt satisfied and relieved that the two suitcases for Prince John were already loaded aboard the floatplane, and everything should click into place in the next 48 hours, once his fishing week had drawn to a close and he returned to London.

He just had to double check the biometrics had been uploaded from the fishing rod he'd given Prince John, so the ECG signature could be transmitted when required.

Chapter 17

Dave could hear the commotion outside and had looked at the unfolding scene through a narrow slit in the curtain. Donald and his son were among the villagers confronting the three men, and seeing them win a small victory gave Dave a little hope. But he kept thinking how tough it was going to be to find Mike and get home.

Cathy had made them some brose. Dave had never tried it but liked it so much he wanted to get some when he hopefully got home. Yana wasn't so keen but cleared her plate nevertheless.

Donald brought the van around, and they all got in. Dave was in the back with Bessie, the sheepdog. They planned to search the five miles of moorland to the east of the lodge, which seemed the most likely spot for Mike to be hiding, given the logistics.

After parking up, they made their way to the top of the ridge, which overlooked the estuary. If stopped by Campbell's men and asked what they were doing, Donald would say they were looking for some late lambs that had been missed in the recent gathering and that needed castration. He had put the pliers and elastrator rings in his pocket in case they checked.

From the ridge you could also see the village, and way off in the distance you could just about make out the fishing lodge. The area looked vast and was littered with small lochs and pockets of water. Donald assured them Bessie would be doing most of the work, but it looked a formidable task.

Campbell had had the same idea as them, dispatching three men to the area; one was to stay and observe the village, and the other two were to sweep the hillside for any sign of them.

Donald knew this area well, and Dave and Yana on their own would have been doubling back and getting stuck in the wet peat quagmire. With Donald, it was like walking through a maze with your own map. Dave was heartened that Campbell's men would find it very difficult to cover this area. Bessie just seemed to fly across everything, including what appeared to be water, guided by Donald's whistled commands. It seemed impossible he could make such loud whistles just with his tongue and teeth.

Two hours had passed with no sign of Mike when they sat for a rest on top of a rocky outcrop. You could see the Gumerston loch and river system and the ghillies in their boats with their fishers. It was an idyllic scene, certainly a great shot if you had a camera.

Donald suddenly whispered to Dave to go pretend he was taking a piss. He hesitated for a moment, then went. Bessie had spotted somebody coming and had warned Donald. Yana brought the thermos flask up to her face to cover it and looked away, ready to throw hot coffee into someone's face if necessary. As the man arrived and asked who they were and what they were doing, Donald didn't get up, giving half Gaelic, half English answers to the questions being asked and saying they must be getting on as they had a lot of ground to cover. When he called to Yana by his wife's name, she responded perfectly in Gaelic. Donald was answering all the questions directed at Dave. He clearly didn't have the same faith in Dave's linguistic skills.

Campbell's man moved on, and they all sighed with relief. They probably could have overpowered him, but it would have been a very messy business.

Moving forward across the moor, they could still see two of Campbell's men in the distance. They were the only other people moving out there that day, so they would have to be careful. As they progressed with the search, one figure disappeared from view, but the other was still visible.

Suddenly, Bessie stopped in her tracks. Another dog was on the moor. It was the Doberman, chasing her. The Doberman then stopped, looked at them and ran flat-out in their direction, coming straight at them, right for Yana. It was on top of her in a second, knocking her to the ground, licking her face. She sat up and stared at the Doberman, stroking its head.

'My *milyy* (darling), what has happened to you?' she asked as she felt the makeshift repair Mike had done on the dog's head.

Out of nowhere, Boxer had also appeared and was jumping and going around in circles, as only crazy boxers can, when she saw Dave. Mike emerged from his camouflaged tent, still very stiff from the night before. He couldn't quite believe his eyes. Mike and

Dave hugged. Their bodies were shaking at the relief of being reunited.

'Not dead, then. What took you so bloody long?' quipped Mike.

Donald looked back across the hillside. 'Keep low; we might have been spotted.' It was hard to tell from this distance. Had the man even been looking their way?

Crouching down together, they discussed what to do next.

'We need to move now. We've got to assume they've seen us. Going back to Donald's van would be heading straight for them. We need to get across the causeway,' said Dave.

They all nodded in agreement.

'Dave, the Land Rover is in the quarry. I think they left it there when they thought I'd died in the bog, for the police to find. The battery might be dead, but we could bump-start it down the hill. We'll need to check. It could be booby-trapped!'

'Good job we're a bomb disposal team, then. Let's go and check it out,' replied Dave.

Donald said, 'Follow me. If we go this way, there are some stepping stones through the water where the lochs meet that will get us there quickly, and they will never find them. It will save us fifteen minutes at least.'

Donald was moving as fast as he could. On reaching the gap between the two lochs, he was gasping for breath. He pointed at the rocks that had been laid a long time ago. Some of the rocks were easy to see, others had sunk below the water's surface, and a few were at an angle ready to slip you into the loch. Bessie led with ease; she had obviously done this before. Boxer followed, jumping across the first few stepping stones, followed by the Doberman, but both started swimming when they disappeared just below the surface. The Doberman was following reluctantly, using twice as much effort as she needed to cross the gap, which was nearly a hundred yards across. After a few scary moments, everybody was across and heading for the small quarry, which had been used to produce the rock for the local houses and the very few stone walls that existed.

Donald volunteered to go down first with Bessie, in case somebody was lying in wait. Nobody appeared to be there as he went over to the Land Rover. Everybody was peering over the edge in anticipation. Mike had an arm around each dog. Still nobody. Bessie swept the area, it seemed, in seconds. It was clear.

Dave was quickly beside the Land Rover as Mike and Yana scanned the road from both directions, checking around it, under it, then inside the engine and the cab, with what seemed like precious minutes ticking away. All clear, no booby trap. It made sense if the men had left it for the police to find not to have rigged it. As Dave was preparing to hot-wire it, Mike found the spare key under the seat. Anywhere else in the country, and it would have been long gone, he thought.

Mike turned the key. The Land Rover coughed but didn't start. Being at an angle in the ditch would have drained some of the fuel lines. On trying it again, it sounded a little better but still didn't start. It was now a case of what would happen next: the fuel getting to the engine or the battery running flat. Dave lifted the bonnet again to triple-check the battery leads and other electrical connections were all in place. If it didn't start now, it would be a risky bump-start down the hill. It started, it bloody started, spluttering a bit, but keeping the revs high ironed it out.

Dave said to Mike, 'Don't take your foot off the pedal, or it might stall.'

Yana hugged Donald, and Dave said his heartfelt thanks to him and his family.

It was about three miles to the causeway, and Mike wasn't stopping for anybody. He was going as fast as was safe for staying on the single-track road. Yana was introducing herself to Boxer in the back. Dave was looking at the sea against the rocks. The tide was coming in, and it looked fairly high.

As the Land Rover approached the half-mile-long causeway, a lookout could be seen rushing to his van to block the road. Mike floored the accelerator, which rarely made a lot of difference, but going downhill it seemed faster than it ever had before. The van was reversing out to block their path; it was going to be touch and go. Bang, the Land Rover hit the van, scraping all the way down the side and momentarily pushing it onto two wheels. For a long moment, it looked like they were heading into the sea off the causeway, then the Land Rover bounced back, skidded and straightened.

Flooring the accelerator again, Mike headed across the causeway. In the mirror, he could see two figures by the van, but they were not yet getting in and pursuing them. The now-familiar sound of a gunshot rang out. A high-powered hunting rifle this time. The bullet hit the back of the Land Rover, shattering the indicator light and ricocheting through, lodging itself in the metal back of Dave's seat. Yana grabbed both dogs and lay flat. Another shot, and this bullet hit the back-door window, shattering it as it came right through the cab, exiting by the rear-view mirror.

Then nothing. The men were getting into the van in pursuit. Mike could see the van in the wing mirror as he raced across the causeway towards the main island and, hopefully, safety. Then he clocked a clear view of the road ahead and realised the causeway was rapidly disappearing under the water. This was much deeper than when they had previously crossed; then, the water had come up to the tyres. Waves were also breaking across the deepest bit. Not that far now to the main island. They could almost touch it, but were they going to float away into the sea?

The Land Rover ploughed ahead, Mike slowing a little, only to stop the water cascading into the engine. The doughty vehicle then started to float a little, but the momentum was still pushing it forward, albeit at a slight angle. Please, Land Rover, don't cut out, was everybody's silent prayer. Then one tyre touched down, then the others; they had passed the deepest bit. Mike checked the mirror to see where the van was; it was right behind them, but it had started to float and was drifting off the causeway. Their pursuers wouldn't make it. They were across and safe for the moment. A faint cheer of relief rang out.

Chapter 18

Campbell was sitting in his office, getting updates from the different teams he had sent out to comb the countryside.

One had reported a possible sighting on the moor, but it was so far away the scout thought it could have been the crofter they'd talked to earlier, rounding up his lambs.

Campbell had heard nothing from the causeway sentry for a while, so he radioed through. Nothing. He tried again – still the same. He then called the man he'd left to overlook the village. 'Get over there and see what's happening.'

Finn reported in to confirm none of the domestic staff had helped the prisoners escape. Annie was his reliable source who would tell him everything that was going on between the staff members. The message coming back was clear. No one was going to risk it after what Pete had done to Kristijonas. So, it was the other diver.

'You thought he was dead!' accused Campbell.

The radio crackled just as Finn was about to leave. The Land Rover had crossed the causeway. Campbell's fist hit the desk.

Campbell was visibly annoyed. Finn had never seen him like this, in all the time they'd worked together. He needed to act fast, before this got too messy. It would be hard to clean it up and then convince the previously-compliant West Highland Police there was nothing to see here.

Campbell had just eaten lunch with the prince's pilot, Roger Wilson, who was staying in the annex of the main lodge. Roger dined with the lodge staff rather than the fishing guests and was passing his days walking, reading and visiting some of the brochs and standing stone circles. 'Is Roger still here?' Campbell said urgently.

Campbell knew with the tide in and with only the tractor able to get across, they had no chance of catching the group by road. With the Land Rover on the move, there was little time to act. The floatplane was his only option for cutting them off. He had quickly got to know how petty the prince could be, but he needed to borrow the plane before he returned from his day's fishing. Campbell didn't like being obliged to anybody, but needs must, he thought.

Annie had found Roger and was bringing him to Campbell. Roger had a gut feeling this would not be good.

Roger sensed Campbell wasn't somebody to cross without an excellent reason. Campbell explained that one of their vans was out of action and a couple of his men had promised to get some special Harris Tweed made for the chairman of the fishing syndicate. He could tell the prince, if he returned early, that he was doing a scouting trip to get him to the favoured top loch tomorrow, which usually took about two hours by van and boat and also involved two long walks. Roger listened to Campbell, thinking the whole scenario sounded very unlikely.

Roger was rather concerned by the request, as he might get his marching orders if the prince returned to find his precious plane had gone without his permission.

Roger was no fool and had been observing from the fringes the comings and goings at the lodge. Despite the swan-like appearance above the surface, there was clearly frantic activity going on below. Roger decided he was going to do what had been requested. It was an order in all but name.

They were in the air in ten minutes. The cases the men had put on board made the hair on Roger's neck stand up. What the hell was the prince involved in this time? The prince complained of press intrusion, but if they really knew what was going on, it would beggar belief.

The only reason Roger could think of for Prince John insisting his protection officer fly back from Ireland without him was that he was breaking the law again.

Just drop them, come back, lie low for one more day, just one more day, Roger thought. Maybe he could go back to his old job, where he didn't have to compromise himself.

The road on the main island went around the outside rim, from one small village to the next. The first was seventeen miles from the causeway. Campbell looked at the map again; it would be close, but getting two men in position just before the village was possible. They could set up position above the pass that had been recently blasted through the hillside for the new road that now provided half a mile of two lanes – a rarity on the island. It had an excellent line of sight, so the Land Rover would be thoroughly exposed as it approached. He had also placed his best marksmen on board, with orders to kill everybody in the Land Rover and any other car that was unlucky enough to be in the vicinity when the Land Rover was taken down.

If another car was involved, they were to stage a collision and burn the vehicles to cover their tracks. If no other vehicle was involved, they would just drive the Land Rover off the road into the sea. This would not be difficult, as half the road was along the cliff edge.

The two men were quickly in place with gunsights trained on the road, waiting for the Land Rover to come into view.

Chapter 19

It was a massive relief to have made it across the causeway, and even better to know Campbell's gunmen couldn't follow until the ebb tide, which would be in about four hours. As they looked to the road ahead, the bullet hole through the front windscreen stared back at them; a few inches on either side, and one of them would be dead.

Mike got Dave up to speed on what had been happening since he'd jumped out the back of the van: the bog, the dogs, the diversion, and Boxer coming to his rescue at the sea estuary. Dave explained about Poppy, the wreck dive, how close they'd come to getting shot to pieces escaping on the RIB and how Cathy and Donald had helped them.

Yana asked, 'The packages you recovered? Were there two large, heavy bags?'

Dave replied that there were. 'What was in them?'

Without answering, Yana asked, 'Where are they now?'

Mike replied that he'd seen them loaded onto the seaplane. Mike pressed Yana as to what she knew. Just as Yana was about to give her answer, the noise of a plane was heard above them.

It was the distinctive sound of the seaplane. They looked out the windows in all directions to see if it was what they feared. Mike stopped the Land Rover, and Dave got out to see the seaplane disappearing into the low cloud. It dawned on them like a great weight pressing down that this wasn't over. Campbell was using the prince's seaplane to get ahead of them and likely to set up an ambush. They all knew they would be sitting ducks if they went ahead.

Dave pulled the Land Rover over into a lay-by. What were their options? Race ahead and hope they could get through before the ambush was set up? Nobody knew the road well enough to predict where it would be. Reinforce the front of the Land Rover and try to survive a barrage of bullets? But with what?

Dave then piped up, 'There's a mountain pass close by.' He had read about it in the latest Trail Runner magazine. It went from one side of the island to the other, and he'd thought of running it after the job of clearing the mine had finished. It would have made up for missing the Solway run, plus, when on earth would he ever be back here?

Dave looked at the map, finding that the trail was just over half a mile away. The magazine was still in the vehicle, and he described the terrain to the others. The route was about five miles across, with some spectacular but treacherous ridges and some bouldering, particularly on the way down. They might make it in a couple of hours, whereas the road around the island was about forty miles and would take Campbell's men one, maybe two hours to get around after the tide turned in three or four hours. That would give them a least a four-hour start, even if Campbell's men guessed where they'd gone.

'We could get to a landline, get Toby to order some military support and get Poppy safe. I think it's our best option,' said Dave.

Mike nodded. They needed to hide the Land Rover.

They had just passed an old, abandoned croft with a rotting corrugated iron roof. They thought they could hide the Land Rover at the back – not great, but just about the only cover in this open landscape. It wouldn't survive a thorough search but might buy them some vital time.

A car park was positioned at each end of the trail. There was a smaller one at this end, as most climbers and tourists went from the main town on the island and would often double back after having reached the summit.

Dave looked at Yana, who seemed hesitant. 'Are you going to come with us?'

She was quiet for a moment, then nodded.

It was dry that afternoon, but in the Outer Hebrides conditions could change at any time. The light was still good, though. They had to make excellent progress if this was to work. The last thing they needed was to run out of light on the most dangerous part of the trail.

Everybody grabbed what they needed from the depleted kit in the Land Rover, with the dogs finishing the tiny bit of food that was left in seconds. Mike looked for similar sustenance, having not eaten since the day before, but all the ration packs had been used up. He grabbed a solitary, dust-covered cough sweet from the front tray and unwrapped it. Any kind of sugar would be better than nothing, he thought.

As they set off, the dogs couldn't believe their luck. They had been wanting to run for days and were now able to. They headed off on the trail at such a pace they had to be whistled back, which seemed to take an age, but they were clearly having a lot of fun.

The trail was catching the afternoon sun, and the hillside looked absolutely stunning. The path at this stage was moving upwards, but not at a huge incline. The dogs were chasing each other up and down as they progressed.

As the route became steeper, the first of the mountains could be seen. They looked sharp and rugged, towering in places, as if much newer and more jagged than the typical rounded Scottish peak. Were they going to manage it with the dogs? Dave was in his element and probably would have been running by now if he'd been on his own. Yana was moving with seemingly little effort. Mike put this down to her diminutive size, as every step he took seemed to be harder than the last. The dogs had calmed down but were still leading the way.

It was then Mike started to feel light-headed and started to stumble; his body was starting to run out of fuel, and he was struggling to find enough physical energy to move forward. His legs were turning to jelly. He shouted to Dave, 'Have you got any food?'

Dave looked back and could immediately see Mike had hit the wall. He had no food to offer Mike, and trying to get him down the mountainside would put them way behind schedule. Yana said she didn't have anything either, then she checked the pockets of the coat she'd been given to find some tablet in a little bag that Cathy must have put in. She gave this to Mike. As he broke it up and ate it, he knew it would take at least twenty minutes to start feeling normal again, but he was determined not to stop. Mike forged slowly ahead as Dave and Yana watched and supported him.

Thirty minutes later, and with Mike starting to feel vaguely normal, the first jagged ridge appeared. They were going to have to scramble along on all fours using their hands for support from now on. The rocks seemed remarkably rough. Mike wondered how much skin he would lose by the time they finished.

The dogs were starting to need a push up every so often. Boxer trusted Dave and Mike completely and would give anything a go once, but doing it twice was often a different matter. Dave was now leading the group across several hundred yards of the ridge, which was like walking across a jagged, steep rooftop. On the right-hand side lay death, on the left the same, and going back was not an option.

The Doberman was starting to look concerned, but Yana looked at her and dismissed her concerns with a forward hand gesture.

Mike asked Dave, 'Is this the worst bit?'

'Maybe,' came the reply – not exactly the reassurance he was hoping for. Dave followed this up with, 'There are some big boulders on the way down. We'll probably have to carry the dogs.'

Doing this in the winter with a gale blowing, Mike thought, would be suicide. He was very grateful it was summer and pretty dry. The trail then started to level out a bit, and the jagged ridge turned into more rounded mountains. The low cloud had lifted, leaving just a few clouds. The view was spectacular. The Gumerston estate looked far away, but the other side of the island was still not in sight.

There were several dips and rises to come, but none as sheer and long as the first. They made good progress, and then the coastline was finally in view. The wind had got up, making it tougher to move along the trail, particularly during the gusts, but it also made it pretty impossible to land a seaplane. Thank the lord.

The main track down to the car park and the small mobile café were now visible. Dave stopped and said, 'I don't think we can risk going straight down.'

There were no other climbers or cars around, as everybody had left for the day. The café was shuttered and appeared closed. If there was anybody waiting there for them, they would walk straight into them.

'We're going to have to go down another route. Left or right?' asked Mike.

Dave looked at the map. Both ways looked challenging. 'Going right would give more cover from the road,' he said.

Yana said, 'Right it is, then.'

On the final section of the track, there were some enormous rocks. They walked and climbed between some and then made an upward climb before the final descent. Looking down from the final hill, it looked very steep. Getting down without injury was going to be bloody hard. No rope and a thirty- to forty-foot drop onto boulders if they got it wrong. A broken limb was looking like a distinct possibility.

Dave went down first, being smaller and lighter than Mike. Physically, he was much better suited to climbing and had a little rock-climbing experience under his belt. Dave assessed the route, looking for the best grips for the easiest descent. When he reached the bottom, he shouted up, 'We need to make a rope for the dogs.'

They looked at what was available to them. They had a belt, the Harris Tweed coat Cathy had given them, and not much else. They started cutting, shredding, and tying the bits together until they had about twenty feet of makeshift rope.

Boxer was the first to go, with a belt tied around her chest. She was lowered as far as possible and then dropped, with Dave catching her as she fell the last ten feet. Dave untied her and threw the rope back up, as Boxer gave him a look that said she was not doing that again, ever.

Up next was the Doberman, tied up in a similar fashion and ready for drop number two. She was lowered and about six feet down didn't like it at all and madly scrambled back to the top. She was having none of this rock climbing.

Yana looked right at her, straight in the eye, but didn't say a word. The Doberman tried to look away, but Yana gently moved her nose until their eyes met and she got the message loud and clear. Mike lowered her again, and this time Yana climbed down with her. She had her fixed stare locked on the dog as she reassured her it was fine. Look at me. She had done it. Now for the drop. *Thump*, as the Doberman fell the last ten feet. Then a scramble to her feet to look cool and nonchalant. Mike finally crawled and skidded his way down, very inelegantly but safely. The descent was done. Dave was rubbing his lower back from catching the dogs.

A few smaller boulders later, and they were near the road and hopefully a few minutes from a phone. The light was fading fast as they approached the village. On the outskirts, they could see a police house on its own, about two hundred yards outside of the hamlet: a small, white bungalow typical of single police houses dotted around the highlands and islands.

Still hypercautious, but hopeful this was about to all be over, Dave and Mike approached the building as Yana stayed back with the dogs. Being cautious and thorough had kept Dave safe throughout his bomb disposal days, and he wasn't going to stop now.

As they got to the fence outside the police house, an automatic light came on, and as they looked at the police house to see if anybody was at home, the crack of a bullet rang out. Dave fell like a stone. He was hit. Mike ducked for cover, then scrambled back to grab Dave by the collar. He dragged him away as fast as he could, heading for the deep ditch at the side of the road. Mike was pulling and moving as Dave bounced along the trough.

Mike had caught a momentary glance of where Dave had been hit when they were under the automatic light. He had seen blood spurt from Dave's cheek up to his ear, or what was left of it.

Dave was regaining consciousness, but Mike was still dragging him, knowing that although he couldn't see anybody, they were being hunted and needed as much distance between themselves and the hunters as possible. At least the fading light was on their side. Boxer had seen Dave fall and was at their side in a flash.

Almost at the same time Dave had been shot, Yana had felt a poke in her back and heard a voice saying, 'Move to the house, or I will shoot you.' As she was pushed towards the police house, the Doberman was barking and snarling at the man, who was paying her no more attention than he would a terrier. As Yana felt the gun push in her back again, she swung around lightning quick and planted her elbow into the assailant's face, where it bounced off. This man was huge. She kicked at his kneecap and quickly followed it up with as hard a punch as she could muster, straight to his throat. She went to run but was grabbed back by her arm. She kicked him again in the groin but couldn't free herself. He picked her up and promptly slammed her into the ground with enormous force. She was winded, gasping for breath as he flung her into the police house and cable-tied her to the stove rail.

Two armed men were now in pursuit of Dave and Mike as they ran for the shoreline, hoping for some cover. As they got there, all they could see was an open beach.

Dave had blood pouring from the side of his face but was now able to walk, half running, with Mike's arm around him dragging him along. They desperately looked around for any cover. There was something in the distance along the beach; from where they were, it looked like a pile of sticks that had formed on the beach like the edge of a bird's nest. It was covering three-quarters of the beach. They thought it must be washed-up timber, but would it give them enough cover? They would be completely exposed until they got there, but they had little choice. They now had the two-hundred-metre run of their lives.

As they ran across the open beach, they could hear the crack of rifle shots and hoped that was not the last sound they would ever hear.

Boxer was leading the way and got to the stick-shaped objects first. It was hundreds of huge pieces of timber and some shipping containers that must have been lost off a cargo ship in the recent big storm and had drifted ashore.

As they got to the timber, they fell to the sand behind the welcome cover the huge pieces of timber offered and looked for their pursuers. They could see two people, but they were a distance away.

Having caught their breath, they hurdled and ducked between the massive pieces of timber until they made it to the end of the beach. They stopped and glanced back. They couldn't see Yana or the Doberman, just a large rowing boat that appeared to have come from the Russian factory ship on the horizon.

The figures were still following them as they scrambled along the rocky, overhanging shoreline, but they weren't as close as expected. Dave and Mike kept moving along the shoreline, which was now giving them good cover, until they were met with a cliff face completely blocking their way. It was now almost dark, but they could see they were on a tiny beach with a cave at one end under the cliff. They could go no further without swimming, and the waves were breaking hard onto the rocks beyond them.

They hid themselves as much as possible, waiting to jump their pursuers when they finally arrived. Mike was positioned on a ledge above the beach, ready to jump on somebody, while Dave and Boxer were concealed in the mouth of the cave.

Meanwhile, Yana looked around the room she'd been thrown in. An unconscious or dead policeman was slumped in one corner. Under the light, she recognised her captor. It was Aleksei, the Russian who had transported her to Gumerston and ran Campbell's import operation from the factory ship. He really was immense and had thrown her inside despite her best efforts.

The Doberman had followed them into the garden of the police bungalow and was still barking and snarling. Aleksei didn't want the dog to attract the villagers' attention, so he went outside to silence it. He picked up a spade that had been stuck in the ground of the small garden and hit the Doberman full in the face. She yelped and cowered away but then came towards him again in a half-hearted approach. He hit her again even harder. She slunk away, whimpering. Not at all the fearsome dog he'd heard Finn boast about in Russia. He approached the dog again to finish her off. She was now trapped in this small, walled garden, with no route to escape except through Aleksei. As he approached for the kill, a switch inside her flicked. She was going to have to fight for her life or be dead in a moment. She turned and attacked with full ferocity. Aleksei swung the spade, catching her a glancing blow, but she turned and attacked again, her most basic killer instinct kicking in. She was now on top of him and ripping at his hands, which he was protecting his neck with. He was desperately fighting her off when Yana appeared. She had used the heat of the stove to soften the plastic and ply the cable ties apart. She ordered the Doberman to stop. The dog's blood rage was so high Yana feared she would just keep going and ignore Yana. Yana put her hand on the dog's collar, wondering if she might attack her too. The Doberman pulled back a fraction, then stopped.

Yana had some questions for Aleksei. She wanted him alive.

Mike and Dave waited and waited, expecting the fight of their lives at any moment, but no one came. They waited in anticipation for some time and were about to return along the shoreline when they realised the beach was nearly under water. They had been cut off by the rapidly rising tide.

They checked their watches to see when the tide would be at its highest. Could they wait it out where they were? It seemed unlikely, given there might be another hour of it rising.

The early morning light was just breaking through as Mike waded back along the rapidly submerging shoreline, hoping they might be able to wade their way out. He was pushed back by the waves breaking over him, which threw him under the water several times as he grabbed for rocks to steady himself. There was no way out for them along the shoreline. As he returned to Dave and Boxer, the beach was now two feet under water. There were now some big waves smashing against the shore on each side of them. Shit. They were going to have to climb.

The cliff was almost sheer and was dripping wet at the bottom. No way was Boxer going to get up this cliff. Dave grabbed a buoy that had washed up into the cave; it had a length of rope attached that he tied around Boxer, and he placed her as high up as he could on a narrow ledge. If she stayed put, she might be okay; if she fell, she should float. Dave looked at her like it might be the last time he saw her. Despite the last few days, she hadn't seen that face before and didn't like it one bit.

As they put Boxer on the cliff ledge, they saw a bottle that had emerged from the sand when they'd pulled the rope out. Inside was a message from 1956, a little damaged by time but readable, from a man professing his love through poetry for a girl. Dave wondered if he should write a note to his daughter, Poppy. Mike told him not to, as they were going to make it. Dave asked Mike to look after her forever if he fell. Mike nodded, although if anybody was going to fall, he thought it was more likely to be him. Maybe the bullet wound was affecting Dave's balance.

The cliff was about fifty feet high, and they couldn't see an obvious route up. Waves were now breaking hard below their feet.

They started the climb, with Mike leading, as Dave was clearly not at his best. Mike knew he had to stay strong for both of them. As he started up, Mike could see some small ledges where moss and grass had grown and headed towards them, digging his fingers in to give himself some much-appreciated grip that was impossible with the layer of green slime that coated much of the lower rocks. Mike checked on Dave's progress. Dave was still with him. They climbed as if in slow motion, knowing that as they got higher, they needed to still have the strength to keep going. When they got up the first section, they stopped on a narrow ledge for a breather. At least no seabirds were attacking them to defend their nests so far, although a few dozen birds were swirling close, probably having a bet on who would fall first. A bit higher up, they found a larger ledge with some daisies, providing them with another brief respite. Looking down, it now looked a very long way. Mike decided not to look again.

A vertical crack in the rock face was now visible and made for a slightly safer and easier climb. Mike wondered if this was what proper climbers called a fissure or chimney. At the top, he could see there were rocks wedged together. Placing a hand on the rock that looked most wedged in place, Mike lifted himself up. Shit. He fell back ten feet, pushing his legs out and grabbing for anything to break his descent. A bunch of rocks and grass bounced off his head and shoulders and then landed on Dave, who had pinned himself to the rock face.

Mike shouted, 'Okay?'

'Yes, okay,' came the reply. The rocks were still very loose at the top of the chimney as he pushed them into the sea below. Mike's arms were now starting to shake, and he feared they might give out but carried on.

They were now just about at the top of the cliff, and Mike could see a grassy covering protruding out over the edge. Mindful of recently gripping bits of heather and them giving way, he grabbed as much of the top as he could. He didn't want to go out and over, but if he pulled at it too vigorously, the grass could give way with him attached. His hands were trembling as he left the certain hold of solid rock and gripped the coarse grass. His heart was racing. He wanted to be anywhere else but here.

As he got halfway up, he saw a man holding out a hand and telling him to take it.

'It's okay,' the man said.

He didn't look like a local but wasn't a face Mike had seen before. He hesitated for a moment. Not knowing whether he was about to be pulled up or thrown off the cliff, he thought, fuck it. He had no more strength. If this was his time to die, then this was his time to die.

The hand gripped his and pulled him clear. As Dave emerged behind him, he looked at the man with equal hesitation, even though he could see Mike standing there.

Yana suddenly appeared beside Mike and confirmed to Dave that it was okay to take the man's hand. She looked different. It was time to update Mike and Dave.

Yana explained that she worked for MI6. She'd been called in by her boss after Colonel Bentley had alerted him to what he thought was going on. Colonel Bentley had realised too late that Campbell wasn't all he seemed. Colonel Bentley had been asked at his club if he could acquire a very select, illicit item. When he questioned why they were coming to him, it had emerged that Gumerston was the place this could happen. Campbell hadn't banked on his clients being so indiscreet.

Yana had interrogated Aleksei about the last shipment and what was in the cases loaded onto Prince John's seaplane. The Doberman had played her part.

She had then made contact, with her two backup agents, whose task had been to shadow her. They had lost contact with her when she was locked up at the lodge. They had just arrived and used their drones to find Mike and Dave along the shoreline.

Yana had also called Poppy's school, getting the housemistress out of bed in the middle of the night to make sure Poppy was safe. A Russian dance teacher was helping them with their enquiries, having being instrumental in setting up the screen test.

Yana went on to say they had a problem that needed Mike and Dave's help, if they were up for it.

'First let's get Boxer up,' said Mike.

Neither Mike nor Dave had the strength to get her, so one of the agents backed the Land Rover to the cliff edge, dropped a rope and abseiled down the cliff, picking up a very wet Boxer from the ledge where they had left her.

Yana explained that the prince was carrying gold antiquities in the two large cases to pay off a Turkish pasha he'd lost money to gambling with. Campbell had offered to arrange the payoff, in the artefacts the pasha had specified, which had been plundered from Troy by the Russians four hundred years ago, if the prince gave him unconditional authority over who he could give half a dozen knighthoods to.

What the prince didn't know was that there was a bomb in the base of one of the cases set to go off when he got to London.

'How do you know the Russian's telling the truth?' asked Mike.

Yana pointed to Aleksei, who was covered in blood and getting first aid from one of the agents.

'We've also had an undercover officer feeding us intel from inside the Russian faction we suspect.'

'Okay. Do you know what type of bomb we're dealing with?' asked Dave.

'We're not certain but fear it's chemical – maybe something close to Novichok, based on recent attacks. You may remember an incident about four years ago that was all over the news.'

The Russian, Aleksei, had strict handling instructions, which would suggest it was very dangerous. So that was why I was diving alone to retrieve it, thought Dave.

'Who's doing this? Surely it's an act of war if it goes off in the centre of London?' said Mike.

'It's been traced back to a hard-line faction in Russia that suffered huge losses in the recent war. They blame the UK for supplying the weapons. At this stage, we don't know if they're acting alone or with the state's approval. We do know that this would be catastrophic if it went off.

'We have to stop them getting to London, so we need to take them down at the Gumerston fishing lodge.'

Dave asked, 'Is this the whole crew?'

Yana answered, 'Yes, but these two guys are as solid as they come. We could fly in our own bomb guys, but we need to move fast.'

Dave said, 'You get us the cases. We'll assess them and defuse if possible. But I'm getting sodding tired of being shot at.'

Yana gestured them towards the new black Land Rover Defender her backup agents had arrived in. 'Will the dogs fit in?' enquired Mike.

At that moment, Boxer came walking up, not at all impressed at having been left behind. 'I know that look. She's not going to forgive us for days,' Dave said.

Richard had bandaged Aleksei and locked him up in the police house cell along with the dead policeman for later collection.

'It's the last day of the week's fishing. We should have until 5 pm,' said Yana, as they all squeezed into the new Land Rover.

Mike asked, 'Yana, is that your actual name?'

She replied, 'Let me introduce you to Tom and Richard, and I'm Harriet, but we go by Tom, Dick and Harri. We often get assigned together.'

As they drove the two-and-a-half-hour journey around the island back to the fishing lodge, Dave used their satellite phone to ring Poppy. She was very excited about a screen test she'd done, and Dave wasn't going to shatter her excitement. 'I'm sure it was brilliant,' he said. Maybe one day he would tell her.

Mike briefed the agents on the lookout points and the approach he had taken to free Dave and Harri.

As they approached Gumerston, the agents prepared themselves and got the spy drones ready.

Chapter 20

The cloud was broken overhead, and the sun was streaming through as Colonel Bentley selected a silver stoat's tail fly to attach to his leader. He'd had good fortune with this fly before in these conditions and was already anticipating the take.

As he cast just above the first lie in the pool, his line landed with a little slack, and as it started to drift round, he mended his line. It was fishing beautifully. Any moment now, he thought. His hand was set, poised to strike.

It was one of the rare moments that week when he hadn't been thinking about his conversation in the Foreign Office and waiting for something to happen. He'd briefed his old army compatriot, Ash Barnes, on his suspicions about what he thought was going on at Gumerston. He'd felt completely confident when he left, certain that it was going to be actioned. Then, nothing.

'Just go on as normal, and we'll deal with it,' had seemed sensible at the time but was becoming particularly frustrating several weeks later. Had it been signed off to some junior who had no interest? Had they forgotten about or dismissed it? He was going to phone Ash a couple of days ago to get an update, but the storm had cut the landlines. He'd even made some excuse to get to the next village by asking for some special Harris Tweed.

Had the arrival of the young hostess at the start of the fishing season been something to do with the plan? Where was she now? He'd been told she'd been given leave to see a sick parent in the last week. Was that the real reason? He was starting to second-guess everything that happened, and last night's commotion from the church group about poor old Dawson was really spoiling his week's angling. He'd waited all winter to be back on this bit of water.

A fish rose and turned; he felt it for a moment but snatched at it and missed the strike. My god, he thought, I never snatch at a fish. This is really messing up my week's fishing. He cast again. Maybe there was another fish waiting for him at the next lie.

He thought about what would happen when Ash dealt with the issue. Could it be kept quiet, or would it be splashed across the front of the tabloids? Just what the bloody left-wing anti-estate buggers wanted, never mind the SNP. He could see the headline, 'Toffs Snared in Smuggling Ring,' or something even worse. What would his colleagues at his club think? Was this going to be a social disaster?

A salmon then broke the surface of the pool and took his fly; he was in, and the fight was on.

Chapter 21

The plan was fairly straightforward; it had to be, given the time factor. They would use the drones to survey the lodge and make a two-pronged attack. One agent would go in along the seawall, and the other two were to go over the hill and through the woods, as Mike had done.

Mike and Dave were to stay put in the Defender with the dogs. There was one gun between them, which Harri had reluctantly given up.

They needed to move fairly quickly to enact their plan before the fishers returned at 5.30, to avoid any collateral damage. They usually had more time and personnel for an operation like this, but needs must. Lunchtime seemed an ideal time to strike, as everybody should be together eating in the staff dining room.

As they approached the Gumerston estate, a drone was deployed. It showed nobody at the causeway, which seemed a little surprising. A second sweep was done with infrared, which just showed some sheep resting at the edge of a peat bank.

As they approached the causeway, full body armour was donned by Harri, Tom and Richard, making Mike and Dave feel more vulnerable than they had before.

Arriving at the lodge, there was no sign of the plane! Had the prince left early?

As they approached the dirt-track road leading up to the fishing lodge, they chose to pass the entrance and continue along the road for about half a mile towards some derelict croft buildings that had previously been used to house estate workers. They would be approaching the fishing lodge from over the hillside for better cover. They parked up between the decaying buildings, so the vehicle was out of sight of where Mike had said a lookout could be located. Once stationary, a final check was done. The game was on. A fist pump and they were on their way.

The drone had spotted a figure on top of the hillside, as Mike had predicted.

It seemed an age as they waited in the Land Rover, then through the radio, 'Target A down.' Then silence.

They presumed that meant the lookout. How were they going to tackle the lodge? wondered Mike.

The drone Harri was using showed a large group gathering in the staff quarters, waiting for lunch: kitchen staff, maids and drivers, all chatting or reading newspapers. A quick scan of the rest of the building was showing nobody else.

Harri and Tom took turns approaching the west side of the lodge, as they covered each other. As they got past the outbuildings and to the back of the guest side of the building, they paused. Harri checked through the camera on the drone, which showed that the lodge staff were now all in the dining room eating lunch. Tom confirmed Dick was in position. Harri moved quickly along the side of the building, entered the guest lounge, placed a smoke bomb in the basket of dried peat they used for the fire and took up position, waiting for the smoke alarm to go off, as it duly did.

Tom was positioned below the seawall and observed the staff dining room clear slowly, as some were reluctant to leave their lunch. One of the maids was getting the blame for a cinder dropping on the carpet, as she was the one who had cleared out the fireplace that morning; apparently it wasn't the first time the smoke alarm had gone off.

Several people had brought their lunch plates with them and were still eating. Dick had entered the lodge from the east side and worked his way through each room until he got to the other side of the dining room.

The moment they were all out, Harri and Tom struck, surrounding them with ultra-compact machine guns and ordering them, 'On your knees, hands behind your head.'

As they fell to the ground, Pete grabbed the cook, putting a steak knife to her throat. Harri said, 'Let her go. There's no escape from here.'

Pete dragged the cook towards the door they had just emerged from, and, as he did so, Kristijonas stretched out a leg to trip him up. As he landed on his back, he was met with the cold steel of Richard's machine gun. Kristijonas had a wry smile on his face as Pete was pinned to the ground and cuffed.

'Where's Campbell? Where's Finn?' were the two questions barked out by Harri.

Many of the staff were doing a double take. Was this the Russian hostess that had arrived a few weeks ago?

The cook spoke up, saying Campbell had just left in a small trawler about fifteen minutes ago. Tom then went down the jetty to check; he could just make out the boat, slowly chugging off into the distance. He looked at the jetty again, expecting to see the launch Mike had talked about moored by it, but it was missing. Anticipating the question, a voice came from the group, saying, 'It's been taken away to get repaired.' It appeared that Campbell had escaped.

Harri was told that Finn had gone with Prince John up to the top loch to start the fishing early to make the most of his last day on the best fishing beat. It had been suggested to Prince John by Colonel Bentley that it wasn't good form to do this, as everybody else went the conventional way, which took nearly two hours and involved several boats and walks, but Prince John had no intention of being held to the conventions of people below his station and didn't anticipate returning here to fish in the near future.

Harri separated out the domestic staff from Campbell's ex-special forces guys, who were promptly locked up in the two cold storage rooms along with Calum, Kristijonas, Pete and the housekeeper, who Harri assessed were all too close to Campbell.

Tom and Richard quickly combed the rest of the lodge and the outhouses in case they'd missed anyone. In less than ten minutes, they declared the site clear.

Mike and Dave had heard a lot of what had occurred over the radio. Dave picked up the radio and said, 'I think I know a way of cutting Campbell off if we move fast.'

Harri listened and said, 'Drive to the lodge, pick up Richard, and give it a go.'

Minutes later, they were racing towards Cathy and Donald's house, hoping they were at home and that there were enough boats still in the village harbour to do the job. Screeching to a halt, they found Donald by his fishing boat and explained their plan.

As Donald turned on the harbour distress siren seemingly out of nowhere, a wave of fishermen rushed to their boats. If they were quick, they might just be able to cut Campbell off.

They left the small harbour in a variety of boats, all in line behind the largest one for cover. They could see Campbell's fishing boat in the far distance. It was going to be touch-and-go whether they could intercept him in time. Donald thought it was their one chance for the village to get rid of this blight of a man from their island.

This was a slow-motion interception, as the boats converged at ten to twelve knots. Mike's thoughts went from, they are never going to get in front of Campbell's boat in time to stop him getting to the open sea, to, maybe they just will.

Campbell was at the back of the trawler as he radioed to the Russian factory ship. He was told their men had returned, but not Aleksei. The captain had no intention of sending any more of his men back to find out where he was and certainly no intention of mounting a rescue for him. He'd had enough of being ordered around by that FSB officer, and since he was no longer on board, the captain could now do what was best for his crew.

Campbell had sensed the night before that the dominos were falling and had called his two fishing boats to get him away if needed. Luckily, one had finished dropping off the bales of drugs around the smaller Glasgow ports and had made its way back to Gumerston overnight. Campbell was now heading for the Russian factory ship to make his escape.

The captain of the factory ship's last words to Campbell were, 'Get here by five o'clock; a minute later and we won't wait for you.'

As he got off the radio, Campbell turned around to see the trawler was now surrounded by local fishing boats, and two machine guns were pointed straight at him.

Chapter 22

As Campbell arrived back at the fishing lodge in handcuffs, the staff looked on in disdain, still too frightened to do or say anything. They suspected his tentacles ran far and deep, so a few insults from afar in Gaelic were all that greeted him.

Harri opened Campbell's laptop. She hoped the password she'd previously seen and used before being locked up would still be current. She keyed in the password, thinking that any second it would be rejected, but no, it was opening. A minor miracle after the last few days. She went to Documents, looking for the mother lode, and clicked on the one file marked imports. It seemed the most likely option and had been recently opened. It popped up password encrypted. She then clicked on another file with the same result. All she could find that would open on the hard drive were fishing records and the legitimate lodge accounts.

As she checked the drawers in his desk and the bin under it, she found a recent note regarding the last packages. 'All white goods recovered and dispatched, black goods two lost, PD complete, LC and ES loaded.'

It wasn't hard for her to work out from the initials which guests they referred to.

She knew the IT specialists at HQ would be able to extract more. She had briefly glimpsed the laptop contents before being thrown into the cold storage room and locked away. She saw a list of gifts given to some of the most prominent people in the UK and the obligations that were due in return. Two columns had been marked with 'deceased, without the obligation being fulfilled.' Somebody was going to have to interview the recipients. Harri was just glad she didn't have to do it.

Harri sat Campbell down and started the interrogation. She presented a picture to him of his operation and how it worked, asking a number of questions she already knew the answers to and judging his reaction to each one.

'Can I have a cup of Earl Grey tea, please? I have a rather dry throat,' was his only reply.

Why did the Russians want to set off a bomb in London? Why a member of the royal family? This was the gist of her questioning.

'I'm sure you can work it out,' came his reply.

She thought to herself that the first question was easy; the Russians thought the prime minister was bought and paid for, and then he went and helped in the war against them. It seemed like pure revenge. Harri thought that the irony of this PM, who had lied to everybody else, having any more loyalty to the Russians, whatever they did for him, seemed almost funny. London? Where else? The royal family? To hit them would be a blow to the heart of the crumbling empire in their eyes.

She put that scenario to Campbell, who nodded. 'I presume if you wanted to live, you had no choice but to cooperate,' she posited.

'I would be just another person killed by Russian operatives on British soil. I remember the days when you were safe once you crossed the English Channel.'

Colonel Bentley, having just returned from fishing, was pacing outside the door after Tom had told him he couldn't enter, pouring himself a whiskey to quell his anger. The moment Harri stopped the questioning, he came storming into the room. 'You traitorous bastard. Why have you done this?'

Tom grabbed the colonel's arm as he glared in Campbell's face.

'This country needs to be shocked to its core. A century ago we were the most important country in the world. Now look at us,' was Campbell's reply.

Colonel Bentley threw what was left of his whiskey at Campbell's face in disgust. 'You will pay for this.'

'I'm sure I can rely on my contacts to assist me with this little misunderstanding. I'm sure you know many of them,' Campbell retorted.

'That's if they keep you alive,' Colonel Bentley said as he slammed the door.

Just at that moment, the sound of a plane could be heard. The prince was returning a little late. Tom and Richard were in position to apprehend Finn when he came ashore. One of the ghillies cast the line off the rowing boat by the jetty, ready to pick them up.

Suddenly the plane roared and then rose and swung around, flying over the lodge again.

Finn had seen out of the corner of his eye somebody waving a white tablecloth on the hillside behind the lodge; on closer inspection, he could see it was Annie, one of the chambermaids. He then noticed there was nobody outside chatting, drinking and weighing their day's catch on the outside table, as he would have expected. Something wasn't right.

Finn barked, 'Roger, up.' Roger looked at the prince, who started to say, 'This is my …'

Finn interrupted. 'I think it's the law. Do you really want to explain why you have artefacts from the Pushkin Museum in your cases?'

'Bugger. Bugger. Are you sure? Do a loop.'

As they circled, Finn could now see the tablecloth laid out with a big sign saying, 'Police.'

Annie had become infatuated with Finn, his muscular physique, the fact he would go running with his shirt off. Her friends had tried to warn her about him, but she interpreted this as jealousy and became even more enamoured with him. Finn, for his part, had occasionally given this young woman a kiss on the cheek, which was enough for her to now save her man.

As the plane turned away for a second time, Roger asked, 'Where to? We need fuel.'

They didn't have much left after coming up from Ireland to the Gumerston estate a week ago – maybe a hundred miles in the main tank and eighty-five miles on reserve. 'Barra or Oban,' said Roger.

'They both have small airports where we should be able to get fuel before an alert goes out. If the tide's in, Barra's the better option, otherwise Oban.'

'The tide's on the wane,' said Finn.

'Barra it is, then.'

'Why don't we just dump the cases?' Roger asked. 'We could land back up at the loch on the top fishing beat and hide the bags underwater, then return and bluff it out. We could say we realised we'd left your new rod there by mistake and went back to retrieve it.'

It sounded very tempting and plausible to the prince, but he also knew he'd exhausted his excuses and delayed his huge gambling debts to the point that a story that would finish him was ready to be sent to the tabloids, including pictures, video recordings, the whole bloody lot. Those bloody foreigners wouldn't care about bringing him down; they would probably profit from it.

'We need to head for Barra,' said the prince.

'Are you sure?' asked Roger.

There was no reply, just an ashen-faced prince with sweat pouring down his face. Roger wondered if he was about to have a heart attack.

Annie was now sitting down with Tom and Richard, sobbing. She had done it for the love of her life and would do it again.

Harri fully briefed her boss in London. A helicopter was coming from RAF Lossiemouth to take Campbell for interrogation at headquarters. His instructions to Harri were to secure the artefacts from the other two guests and caution them. 'We'll deal with that problem later. The RAF police coming from Lossiemouth in the helicopter can transport those you have in custody to our Glasgow office in the Land Rover. We need to find out more about the bomb. What's in it? What's the trigger? Push him as hard as you can.'

Harri tried again with Campbell to get details about the bomb. Was it a nerve gas bomb, as Aleksei had said? How would it detonate? What size was it?

She had done the courses and read the books on how to break somebody down. The trouble was, the person who had written some of them was sitting in front of her, looking decidedly unimpressed.

In the meantime, Richard had located the two packages Dave had retrieved from the wreck from the backs of two cars outside the lodge. He unwrapped them to find a painting and a box full of rough diamonds. He briefly interviewed Lord Colbury as to what he'd planned to do with the diamonds. His Lordship apparently had no idea how they had come to be in his Range Rover.

'That's not what it says in Campbell's spreadsheet. Something to do with a referendum, perhaps?' said Richard, bluffing.

The Earl of Strathglen was more defiant. 'I just had to have that painting. It's just so beautiful.'

Richard looked down at the random pieces of paper he was pretending contained the relevant details, and said, 'You were prepared to do this for it?'

'Well yes, half the buggers in the government are doing it,' came the reply.

It seemed an age waiting for the helicopter to arrive, but it had made pretty good time. Two RAF policemen who had arrived with it were briefed about the danger Campbell's men posed and were left to drive them back to the Glasgow office in the Land Rover.

Dave and Mike were going to travel back in the helicopter, in case the prince's plane was spotted and they needed to divert to it. Campbell was taken on board and cuffed to the seat. The huge rotors started to turn, making a low, pulsing noise. Boxer and the Doberman looked at each other. What was this thunderous beast they were in? Richard opened some rations and put them in a bowl for them: chicken and something, so couldn't be too bad.

They stopped briefly on the other side of the mountain range to pick up Aleksei from the police house cell. Harri was glad to see he was still there, but the Doberman wasn't, and as Mike held her collar, she gave out a deep, blood-curdling growl. Seeing Aleksei come on board with blood-drenched bandages was the first time Harri had seen Campbell's ice-cold demeanour change.

Finn's last instructions from Campbell and his Russian handlers had been simple: get the prince and the bomb to London. Thus far, he had used suggestion to get the prince do what he wanted. But at some stage, he knew he would need to use the gun he was carrying.

Roger had been the one to suggest alternative solutions and personally was thinking one overriding thought: how could he get out of this alive? Not getting blamed in some way would also be good. He knew the way of things was to create a scapegoat for the press in order to save yourself. This tactic had worked pretty well in the past for royalty as well as politicians.

Roger wondered if he'd have a chance to escape when they landed at Traigh Mor airstrip on

Barra. It was a tiny airport with little cover; on reflection, he didn't fancy his chances too much.

They were almost there. He was flying as low as possible to avoid radar, but that was making it difficult to pick out the landing strip. All he was seeing appeared to be one small island after another. Roger kept looking for the red windsock by a beach, but there were so many white beaches he wondered if he'd missed it. Barra had the only airstrip where you landed on the sand, which made the approach ideal for a seaplane when the tide was high.

Roger was grateful the conditions were clear as he finally spotted the red windsock and the airport building. It was time to land. The sea was fairly calm, so the bumps over the waves were pronounced but safe. Roger brought the plane around to be level with the end of the very small airport building, which usually catered for no more than a dozen people.

Roger thought if he was left on his own to get the fuel truck, he could just make a run for it. There were only a few people about, and he rated his chances to outrun Finn. Unfortunately, Finn was right behind him as he exited the plane and went to find the fuel truck and what appeared to be the only airport worker around to sign off the payment. As he filled the tank to the brim, he could feel Finn's presence right behind him. There must be another chance at some point to escape, he thought.

Roger filled in the fuel receipt, adding at the end 'SOS' and the number of the plane, and handed it back to the airport worker. They boarded the plane and quickly got in the air. Roger wondered if the fuel man would even notice what he'd written.

As the Chinook flew towards London, Harri was under her headphones, listening for any updates. Nothing on the radar, nothing from the coastguard so far.

Radio messages were constantly being sent to the prince's plane. It seemed either the radio and mobile phones were switched off, or they were just being ignored.

Then a message from Barra. A seaplane had fuelled up, and the pilot had left an SOS message on the fuel receipt.

Harri spoke to the Chinook pilot, and they changed direction. It was a long shot, but if they were in the vicinity when it was spotted, a fighter jet may be able to force it down safely.

Roger was flying as low as he dared along the western coast of Scotland. Finn had been plotting a route for Roger, avoiding any towns and villages, but the weather was starting to close in and the light was fading, making it very dangerous to continue flying that low. They would need to rise up soon, making them visible to radar, or land the plane.

They would be over the border into England soon, with none of the sea inlets that were so numerous on the west coast of Scotland to hide in.

Looking at the map, Finn suggested Ennerdale Water. It was close to the coast and very isolated compared to other lakes in Cumbria. Looking at the map, it appeared to have a single-track road and just a few houses at one end. It should be possible to land and hide the plane behind one of the small headlands.

With the light fading and banks of rain coming in from the Atlantic, Harri decided the odds of somebody spotting the plane were slim and asked the Chinook pilot to change course back to London.

The section chief at Embankment HQ was keen to keep this in-house as much as possible. If Campbell's tentacles spread as widely as Harri was suggesting, he wasn't sure who he could trust in the government, although with such a quick turnover of foreign secretaries this year, that gave him a bit of room for manoeuvre.

He called Alex in, who Colonel Bentley had met with at the start of this operation. 'Yes, everything Harri had relayed has been solidly backed up. The two bomb disposal guys have detailed the cargo that was retrieved. The Russian officer has given some details of the bomb. No, we haven't been able to contact Prince John.'

It was time to call the minister to make the call on the prince.

Alan Bolton listened to what he was being told. He was on holiday in Mallorca. 'Bugger, bugger, bugger.' Why was it him that this happened to?

'Will you let the PM know? We need a decision on taking the plane down before it gets to London.'

'You want to kill the fucking prince?'

'If a nerve gas bomb is exploded in central London, it could kill thousands and take weeks to decontaminate, never mind the immediate call to retaliate. It could become a monumental mess very quickly. An unfortunate plane crash, on the other hand, might not be so bad,' said the section chief.

The message was clear. 'No fucking way' was the PM going to give that order. Go down as the PM who ordered the death of the prince? Not a chance. Some bastard was sure to leak it.

'Tell that man he has to find another way. Tell him to radio the plane, saying no charges will be brought against Prince John. Find out who he owes money to and see if we can apply some pressure there.'

Shit, Bolton thought, it's going to be my head on the block if this goes tits up.

As the plane approached Ennerdale Water, there was little in the way of light from houses, and with the cover of the hills, Finn was fairly confident they were undetected. Even though they'd just crossed the M6 motorway, he doubted anybody was paying the slightest attention. The plane came in to land halfway down the lake, touching down with little fuss apart from scaring the life out of a group of teenagers who were doing their Duke of Edinburgh Award, canoeing through the lake on the way to the youth hostel just over the hill.

The prince had said little the whole trip. His mind was churning between getting these gold artefacts to London to clear his debt and dumping the whole lot in the lake and being laid bare across the tabloids. Deep fake; he could say it's deep fake, brazen it out. Another voice in his head was saying, you need the money. He owed money to friends, family and some sycophantic hangers-on he'd promised titles and access to.

He thought it very poor form that the Turkish cove actually wanted him to honour his debt. He felt the world was against him. Any other prince would be able to sell land and palaces and have more money than god.

Roger was still calculating how to get out of this. Could he just make a dive for it in the middle of the night and swim to shore?

'I think we have four hours of dark, and then we can get back in the air, land near London and offload these bags.'

Finn looked at the map and asked the prince, 'Where could we land?'

'Bobby. We could land at the back of Bobby's house and drive in.'

Roger knew the lake he was talking about; it was more like a very large pond in a valley. 'Too dangerous, Sir,' was Roger's reply.

'Really? I'm sure somebody did it.'

'Yes, it was the Red Rooster stunt team at the start of the horse trials. This is no stunt plane, Sir.'

'How about Pippa's house near Henley on Thames? They have the private island with the tennis courts, with nobody overlooking them, which is a miracle that close to London.'

'Their old wooden launch may be moored out front, but I think it's the best option,' said Roger.

'Pippa's it is, then,' said Prince John, as Roger starting working out the best route.

'We can still just put the bags in the lake and pick them up later?'

Silence. At least he'd tried.

The prince called Pippa, and, after a long delay, he finally got a connection. 'This is a terrible line. I can barely hear you.'

'I'm in a tent in Botswana.'

'Shooting elephants, eh?'

'So bloody funny, John! No, meeting up with a new diamond supplier. Do you know what time it is? What can I do for you, Johnny boy?'

'I need to park my seaplane by your Henley house tomorrow morning.'

'What the hell's going on? If this comes back to bite me, I swear, I bloody swear …'

'Just a small misunderstanding. It'll all be sorted out tomorrow.'

Pippa listened, not believing a word and knowing he would do it anyway, whatever she said.

The Chinook had made good time as it approached Greater London airspace on the way towards the Thames. Mike and Boxer had managed to get some sleep, but every time Dave started to doze off, the Doberman would let out a low growl towards

Aleksei. Harri was still hoping to hear some news as they came in to land at Battersea Heliport. A short ride and they would be at headquarters on the Embankment.

The more Harri thought about the spreadsheet of names and obligations, the more worried she was about getting them back for interrogation. As they landed, Campbell and Aleksei were hooded. If there was a sniper, at least it would be a fifty-fifty chance. The fading evening light would give them good cover. Harri ordered any surrounding lights to be turned off.

The noise as the Chinook landed was disorienting. They left the helicopter in defensive formation, as if she was landing in hostile territory in Iraq.

Two grey vans were waiting for them. Harri emptied them of personnel and split her team across both vans. Maybe it was watching too much TV, or increased paranoia through lack of sleep, but nobody was getting ambushed at the eleventh hour on her watch. They arrived ten minutes later at HQ by a somewhat convoluted route.

The light was starting to break through the clouds as Roger looked at his watch. 3.54 am. The valley was still very dark, but the sky was brightening.

It would be sunrise in half an hour. They needed to go now if they wanted to get there as covertly as possible.

He checked with the prince. Was Pippa's house still the destination?

'Let's go.' The prince seemed in good spirits. 'Keep low, so those buggers don't find us.' This nightmare is nearly over, he thought. No more gambling with sodding foreign strangers from now on.

They took off from the dark lake with fingers crossed that there were no floating tree branches to hit. As they lifted off, two hours and I am safe, the prince thought. Roger kept the plane low, half expecting that at any moment a fighter jet would appear behind them and tell them to land. Nothing was appearing, but he kept looking. Were they just waiting for him to land in the lake at the prince's official residence?

What was in those heavy bags? Did they know Finn was on board? Were they just giving him a free pass because he was royalty? How many times had that happened to him already?

He had landed at Pippa's place before, and it was tight at the best of times, when they'd deliberately cordoned it off. What if there was a boat or some early morning rowers about? As they approached, it seemed clear, and he took the plane straight down, landing it with a bit of a bump and a lot of engine noise to bring it to a stop quickly. He hastily manoeuvred it into the covered harbour in the woods, where the plane could be hidden. He tied up.

Roger had decided this was where he had to make his move. He knew the area well and knew Finn would have to help him move the bags, as they were so heavy. One dry run with the first bag, he thought, and then run to the woods and dive in the Thames when he got the chance.

The first bag was unloaded and taken up to the garage by the tennis courts and manicured green lawn; the second case was halfway up when Bert, Pippa's house sitter, appeared in his dressing gown, with a shotgun aimed straight at them.

Finn stopped to feel if his gun was still in place. Bert looked straight at Prince John and lowered the shotgun. 'We weren't expecting you, Sir. Pippa's still in Africa.'

'Just back from fishing in Scotland. Thought I'd drop her off a couple of salmon.'

'It looks like you caught a ton's worth, if they're in those bags.'

'Oh, just some presents from Ireland. Thought we could leave them here and pick them up later.'

'Does Pippa know? Why don't we put them in the back of the Range Rover? You can send somebody to return the vehicle later.'

Bert put the shotgun down and asked Prince John if he could make him a cup of tea.

That was the moment Finn took out his gun and shot Bert dead. Roger ran for his life across the lawn to the Thames. Prince John seemed in shock as Finn raised his arm and pulled the trigger, the bullet striking Roger as he dived into the water.

Finn told the prince to pick up the case and help him lift it into the boot of the Range Rover. As they carried it towards the vehicle, the prince dropped it and ran. Finn picked up Bert's shotgun and fired it, hitting the turf immediately in front of the fleeing royal, making him pull up sharply as he slipped on the grass, landing on his backside. Finn stood over the prince, kicking him hard in the stomach as he gasped for breath. Finn then picked him up by the throat and threw him towards the vehicle, making him lift the case into the boot. He told him to get into the driver's seat of the Range Rover and placed the cold steel of the pistol into his neck.

'I've got the money for the pasha. I've got the money; it's in the cases.' Then the realisation came that Finn wasn't working for the Turk. 'What do you want? Are you robbing me?'

'I just want you to drive to Buckingham Palace. I think you know the way.'

As they moved off, Finn made a call on his phone. 'Operation Hammer is go. ETA forty minutes.'

Roger felt the bullet strike just before hitting the water. His arm felt like it was on fire, but he had dived and kicked hard towards the tree roots. Expecting to get shot at again any moment, he remained under the water as long as he could, just popping his nose above the water and breathing out as slowly as he could. He stayed there for what seemed an age but was only about fifteen minutes. As he slowly lifted his head up, he could see a body on the grass. The Range Rover was gone.

He rushed to Bert, but he was dead. That could have been me, he thought. Going into the kitchen, he picked up the phone, called the police and told them what had happened.

'A Russian has kidnapped Prince John. Is that what you're saying, Sir? You know it's an offence to waste police time.'

'There's a body here, you bloody idiot.'

'No need to be offensive, Sir. We will send a police car round in due course.'

He didn't believe them. Roger phoned the palace number and waited; he knew it was early, but no reply, really? He phoned for an ambulance this time. 'Someone has been shot?' They were coming immediately, thank goodness.

Chapter 23

As they disembarked from the van, they were greeted by Harri's boss, Simon, who ushered them in with some additional security. 'I hear you've had a rough few days. We'll need a debrief now while it's still fresh in your mind, in case we missed anything vital.'

Simon kneeled down and greeted the two dogs with some treats. 'I hear you two have been having a big adventure,' he said to them as he stroked their heads.

Another man came over to them and gave them some more treats. This is good, they thought, just like going to the … Shit, it's a vet!

'Just a few stitches and a bit of bandaging,' the man said to Simon.

Aleksei was holding up his hands, which had bandages on seeped through with blood. 'Fucking English. You care more about your bloody dogs.'

Simon signalled for a medic. When he arrived, Simon said, 'Get Dave Scott sorted out first and then the Russian. Tell Chris I want him lucid for questioning.'

Two other men took Campbell up the stairs to a holding room. 'Tell Alan Bolton I want to speak to him,' was all he said.

They made their way up into the building. Simon opened the doors to a large meeting room.

Harri enquired whether there was any news about the prince's plane. Simon replied, 'Nothing since Barra. We have surveillance at his country residence and a couple of likely stately homes with lakes near London. We know the Russian known as Finn is with them. That was confirmed by Barra Airport, and there was an SOS note from the pilot, but no destination.'

'So, they're probably making it up as they go,' said Harri.

'We have RAF on alert for the plane if it's a 9/11 scenario, but the fuel explosion would likely destroy any toxins released, so we don't anticipate that,' said Simon, as he left to debrief Mike.

Mike recalled as much as he could of what he'd seen at the fishing lodge, then stopped after fifteen minutes to ask for some food. They seemed to know most of what he was telling them already. He presumed Harri must have relayed what he'd told her to Simon. This was just going over old ground. Then Simon stopped. 'A rod. They gave him a new fishing rod. What about the handle? Was it any different?'

'Maybe. It looked dark, not the usual light-brown cork colour, but I couldn't be sure at that distance. Why, what's the significance?' asked Mike.

'Biometrics, fingerprint recognition, but certain royal locks have been updated to use an ECG recording as a signal to open some royal residence entrances, maybe even set off a bomb?' Simon ventured.

Harri entered, then left with Alex to interrogate Aleksei, who seemed to be the better bet for getting information from, although without an angry Doberman it might prove more difficult.

Dave returned from the medical centre with both the dogs.

'I need a photo,' said Mike, taking out his phone, which he had recovered from the fishing lodge, and snapping the three of them covered in bandages.

'What about the ear?' asked Mike.

'A graft or a false one,' said Dave. 'They apparently take the graft from your ribcage. Weird.'

Dave sat down and grabbed some food. He took a few mouthfuls before he looked at Mike. Yes, they were not wasting the taxpayer's money on the food here.

Aleksei was proving much less cooperative in this environment and was playing by the standard textbook. Yes, he would go to jail here for a while before an exchange was arranged.

Harri left Simon to it, wanting to check up on any new intel. She surveyed the massive screens on the operations wall in room 3. They covered most of London. It all looked very impressive; number plate and facial recognition was everywhere in Inner London. John, the IT operations manager, was confident that any vehicle would be picked up. He talked about the impressive results they'd had in previous operations.

Harri was more sceptical. Rogue terrorists were one thing; a veteran Russian operative was another.

Harri went back to the meeting room. 'We need you guys to stay for the moment, but we'll get you on the road as soon as possible.'

Mike and Dave, in unison, replied, 'We want to see this through. Those bastards tried to kill us. We're not going anywhere. Use us if you can.'

Harri sat to join them for some food, making a fuss over both dogs, who were now her best pals, and feeding them the occasional titbit from her plate. Having the dogs there was a good antidote for her stress levels, she thought.

'Have you got a dog at home?' asked Dave.

'No. I move around too much, but my parents have a couple of retrievers.'

It then it suddenly struck Mike, seeing Harri more relaxed on her home turf and the light making her hair look lighter. Had he met her before at a motorcycle racing school in Pembrey, Wales? Maybe. He asked. 'Do you ride a Honda SP2 twin?'

'Yes, why?'

'Did you do the superbike school at the national circuit in Wales? I think we met.'

'Oh wow, yes, you had some scary blue leathers.'

'Scary leathers?'

'Yes, it looked like you'd slid down the track on them a few times,' Harri said.

'You have to push it to get to your limit,' Mike said, trying to sound macho. Then, remembering where he was and who he was talking to, he instantly regretted it.

'It was so wet that day; everybody thought they would cancel the race meeting at lunchtime, but they just got another ambulance on standby!'

'They would have had to give us all our money back otherwise. What are you riding now?' asked Mike.

'I love the SP2 for track days, but I just got a brand new Blade. It's in the car park. Unless it's been nicked while I've been away.'

'Safest place in London, I would have thought.'

'Simon had his Ducati nicked last year right from the front of the building, but he's upgraded the security since then.'

'London bike thieves are cheeky bastards,' said Mike.

It was good to talk about something normal for a change, thought Harri.

'Maybe we could go for a ride together when this is over, or walk the dogs,' Mike ventured.

Simon entered the room before Mike got an answer. He was with Tony, who he introduced as their tech boffin and who took them to the biohazard store and gave them the suits and breathing apparatus they could use to defuse any chemical bomb. Simon wanted to keep this in-house if possible, and they had offered.

Dave had used most of this kit before on training courses, but seeing it in front of him sent a chill down his spine as he remembered the images of nerve gas victims in recent incidents.

Dave spoke to Harri as he took the kit down to one of the black vans. 'We want to be in on anything that goes down. You will get us?'

'Are you absolutely sure? This could be very bad.'

Dave nodded. 'Any news yet?'

'Nothing. I don't think anything will happen till the morning. Get your head down. There are some sofas next to the basement gym you can kip on, plus some showers. I'll get you some clean gym kit. The dogs can crash in there too.'

As they went downstairs to find the sofas and showers, Dave said to Mike, 'If we manage to survive this, there are a couple of underwater packages I need to retrieve for Cathy and Donald.'

'Great idea,' replied Mike as he spotted the shower room and grabbed a towel.

As the water fell on Mike's head, he closed his eyes and had vivid flashbacks from the previous days that startled him.

It was good to have a shower and get some clean clothes on, Dave thought as he lay down on the sofa, putting his head down on the armrest and quickly turning over. He was going to have to get used to sleeping on one side.

The dogs sniffed around the room and were soon sneezing from the overpowering smell of spray deodorant. They were also disappointed to only find a meagre offering of apples and oranges in a bowl.

Chapter 24

They just seemed to get off to sleep when there was a loud knock on the door. New intel: 'It's happening.' They rushed down to the operations room where Simon and John were. 'The prince's pilot has been found. He's been shot but called in from a house in Henley-on-Thames.'

'The Russian had taken the prince off in a black Range Rover with the packages. We've got the vehicle details; it's registered to Pippa Hunt.'

John found the licence number and ran the plates through the IT system. The seconds ticked by, then the system picked the vehicle up. It had run some traffic lights just outside Henley at 6.23 am, nearly hitting another car.

'There are two occupants; the prince is driving, and there's no facial recognition on the other person.'

'That's Finn,' said Harri.

'They seem to have stopped for a while between there and the next camera,' said John.

'Fuck. They're on the A4 just coming up to Kensington. They're nearly bloody there,' said Simon.

As they watched the screen, John was on the phone dispatching the nearest police car to intercept.

They could now see from the camera feed that the Russian was driving with what appeared to be the prince slumped in the back seat.

The police officers were getting near the end of their night shift when the call came in. Intercept the vehicle and make a hard stop. It sounded deadly urgent, and their adrenaline was suddenly pumping. They weren't far away, as they were already driving towards Kensington. They scanned the oncoming lane. At least at this early hour, they should be able to pick up the vehicle easily. They were on Cromwell Road when the Range Rover passed them. Slamming the brakes on and turning, they were in pursuit.

As they got behind the Range Rover, they looked for the best place to make the hard stop. It was a pretty open road all the way to Hyde Park, apart from when it narrowed near the French Consulate. They would try to do it there, although without backup it was going to be a tough ask. As they radioed in their plan, Finn slammed the brakes on in the Range Rover. They barely reacted in time to avoid smashing into the back of the vehicle and were now level with the Range Rover as it knocked them into the metal gates at the French Consulate, turning the car over.

Harri ran to the front of the building. She knew it was only about ten minutes before Finn would be in front of Buckingham Palace. She had looked at the screen showing the positions of the other police cars, knowing that they had little chance of getting there and stopping him in time.

This was not going to happen on her watch.

She vaulted down the front steps, shouting at the attendant to open the gate. Her Honda Fireblade motorcycle was still there. She was on it in seconds. It was do or die time as the steel gates ground slowly open.

She could make it. She was sure she had a chance. The Fireblade started to wheelie as she opened the throttle over Vauxhall Bridge: fifty, seventy miles an hour in seconds. She braked and weaved as she hit the traffic crossing at Millbank, then opened the throttle again. The road was flat and straight for a bit. She was now travelling at over 100 mph.

Dave, Mike and Tom were following as best they could in a black van. The dogs, woken from their slumber, were at attention. Something big was happening as they dug their claws into the van floor to stop themselves from skidding.

Harri was now at Victoria Station. The one-way system would take her a longer route. Seconds could be vital, so she crossed the paved island, brushing a couple of pedestrians who were about to cross the road. She gunned it again as she rode down the bus lane, avoiding the ongoing traffic. A bus was dead ahead. She swerved onto the pavement; she was nearly there. Harri then hit the first heavy traffic as the road narrowed and the bus lane disappeared. Roadworks, shit. Braking as hard as she could, the rear wheel of the bike lifting off the ground, she crashed through the plastic barrier onto a lane with no traffic, just missing the large open hole they had started digging in the road. She was seconds away as she passed the Royal Mews then the Victoria Memorial in front of Buckingham Palace.

As she desperately looked for the Range Rover, she saw it staring right at her, dead in front. She had no time to get off the bike and shoot the tyres. She calculated that she had one chance: swing the bike round in an arc and let it go, so it wedges itself underneath the car. As she spun it round, her knee touched down on the tarmac first, followed by her elbow as she separated from the superbike. It was sliding straight for the Range Rover, hitting it and jamming itself underneath. Harri was flung towards the railings.

Tom was driving the black van flat-out, smashing the wing mirrors off on pillars and passing trucks. Braking and hitting the pavement as he pushed it as fast as he could. The dogs bounced about with Mike in the back, trying to hold on to them. The van had just passed the Royal Mews when they hit gridlock from two cars that had crashed, avoiding Harri. They couldn't get through. They were a few hundred yards away as Dave opened the back door, got out and started running. The dogs were right beside him.

Harri had skidded off across the pavement, just missing a steel bollard, and was sitting in a flower bed. She stood, her firearm out; she was heading towards the Range Rover. Finn was looking back at her from behind the steering wheel. She fired multiple shots at him. She paused and looked at the vehicle. Perfect cluster, she thought. Then the realisation: fucking armoured glass. Finn got out as she raised her gun again. *Click*. She pulled the trigger and fired the one shot she had left at his torso. He was still standing. Finn looked her in the eye and smiled as he raised his gun.

She stared at him, frozen. Most of this seemed to be happening in slow motion.

Finn was then hit simultaneously by both dogs, each with their own grudge, and he crashed to the ground. They were on him and showing little mercy. Mike and Dave pulled them off. Tom grabbed and handcuffed Finn. The prince was still in the back seat, tied up and looking the worse for wear as Mike checked on him and removed the seat-belt straps that he was bound with.

Dave swung the back of the Range Rover up and carefully opened one of the cases. The lid seemed unusually heavy, which seemed odd. He removed about twenty gold artefacts, putting them to one side as he carefully cut into the section below to reveal a circuit with a large box underneath it, which appeared to be filled with C4 plastic explosive. Dave looked for the trigger mechanism. No mobile phone attached, so it's activated by a radio signal like you would use to trigger an automatic door or gate.

The prince had gathered himself together, and, as everyone was preoccupied with the bomb, he had decided to scarper to the palace. He fumbled in his pockets for his key fob to open the security gate. He found it and took it out. Mike shouted at the top of his voice, 'Drop it! Drop the key!' but the prince ignored him as he continued hurriedly hobbling towards the palace.

As the prince started to raise the key fob, Harri picked up Finn's gun, took aim and squeezed the trigger.

The bullet hit the prince's hand, sending the key into the air. Everybody seemed frozen, waiting for the bomb to explode. Dave was staring at the receiver in the bomb casing, expecting a green light … nothing. As the key landed, it turned green. Dave looked at the bomb, expecting it to be the last thing he saw, but nothing. Then the realisation came that it had just armed itself. It was on a timer.

He scanned the circuit, assessing what was in front of him. No digital read-out, just capacitors, a variable resistor and an integrated circuit. He put his screwdriver into the variable resistor, turning it to full resistance. That would give him thirty seconds, maybe a minute, he thought. Looking at the circuit, he assessed what he was working with. Five to ten minutes is usual for these devices, he thought. It made sense. The key fob arms the device as they enter through the palace gates but delays until they get to the inner quad before blowing the whole place up.

They were suddenly surrounded on two sides by armed police bearing down on them.

Harri and Tom tried to control the situation as sirens wailed and nervous fingers touched triggers. Too many people shouting. Blocked cars sounding their horns. It sounded like they were at the gates of hell rather than the gates of Buckingham Palace.

Dave blocked out all the commotion as he called Mike over, raising a can of spray freeze and pointing to a mercury tilt switch. Mike knew he needed to spray and keep spraying to freeze the mercury inside. There was also a vibration switch attached to the bomb.

Dave unscrewed the circuit casing from the box, lifting it as gently and evenly as he could, and looked underneath. Four wires led to the detonator, but the circuit had been glued to the small box he had just lifted, obscuring which terminals they were attached too.

The din subsided somewhat as the police tried to clear the area. Percentages were flying through Dave's head of different scenarios for stopping the timer. He couldn't disconnect the power unit, as it was soldered to the circuit. There was only one viable option.

As he held the circuit steady, he pointed to two wires and to Mike. 'You need to cut them simultaneously.'

Mike picked the snippers up and put them on the wires, knowing a fraction of a difference in time cutting through would likely make the bomb explode. He felt the snippers touch the plastic coating on each wire and then firmly cut through.

Dave saw the green light go out. 'It's safe.' He closed his eyes and let out a deep breath. He knew that was the closest he'd ever been to death while defusing a bomb.

They both sat on the ground with their hands over their faces like they might have done at the end of a marathon. Mike was shaking now as tears rolled down his face. He fist-pumped Dave. Harri's and Tom's fists joined them.

Both dogs, who had been standing like statues, as tense as everybody else, were joining in. They were getting stroked and hugged. Then both dogs raised their top lips as they would to sneeze or snarl, and it dawned on Dave that it could be a dirty bomb with radioactive pellets or powder under the C4. The dogs could sense so much more than people.

Levering the front of the box off, sure enough, there were pellets layered between the C4.

Somebody else could deal with that, Dave thought as they cordoned off the area.

Prince John had been taken into the palace. Harri wondered if he would escape justice. Tom said to Harri, 'Bloody hell, that was close; we made that by a dog's whisker.'

As they walked back to the battered van, Harri said to Mike, 'Fancy walking the dogs on Sunday?'

The End

Made in the USA
Middletown, DE
11 June 2024